BLACK SCARFACE

3

"The Wrath of Face"

Jimmy DaSaint

BLACK SCARFACE 3

Published by DASAINT ENTERTAINMENT
Po Box 97 Bala Cynwyd, PA 19004
Website: www.dasaintentertainment.com

For Jaiden

You are my inspiration…

I am the punishment of God,
If you had not committed Great Sins,
God would not have sent a punishment
like me upon you.

-Genghis Khan

Chapter 1
November 18th 2007
Philadelphia, PA...

Inside of her downtown real estate office, Tasha sat helplessly at her desk watching as Face paced back and forth. Seeing the hurt and anger inside of his eyes she decided that it was best to remain silent. Face had his head down as his mind raced with thoughts. He couldn't believe that his personal financial advisor, Peter J. Greenberg, had robbed him for five hundred million dollars; and then was able to disappear without a trace. Face kept picturing Peter living a life of luxury and peace on his dime. The thoughts of how he was manipulated by Peter for years fueled his anger and made him crave revenge. He had felt played and disgusted within himself because he trusted Peter. He had always trusted his instincts and been able to pick up on the phonies but Peter had outsmarted him.

Abruptly Face stopped pacing and walked over to his beautiful wife Tasha. He grabbed her hands and stared deep into her eyes, and he could see and feel her concern and worry. After a long sigh he said, "I can't believe it! I can't believe Peter did this shit to me. How could I have missed the damn signs...I trusted that no good son-of-a-bitch with all my damn money!" Tasha was quick to respond, "Baby, everything will be okay. The real estate company is doing extremely well. In just a few years our company will be well worth a hundred million or more. We will be just fine, besides we are not broke; we just don't have what we had."

Tasha continued to offer a soothing hug and shoulder rub to Face in hopes to comfort him. She wanted her husband to keep his cool and didn't want him to snap. It was clear that Peter didn't take a few hundred thousand; he had taken the bulk of their fortune, which allowed them to live a life that was more than simply comfortable. Face wanted to be on top and to make sure any children and future generations in his family would inherit their wealth. Now with that vision and possibility hanging in the balance, Tasha knew she had to play it cool to keep Face from making any foolish mistakes out of anger.

"I'm not going to rest until I find Peter…and when I find him I'm not going to rest until I crush him like he never even existed. He crossed me! He done got me to that point…I mean I'm sick of everyone who has ever fuckin crossed me. Everyone who thought it was gonna be okay to sit back and wish I was in a cage or the grave." Tasha looked at Face and said, "Baby please calm down. Stress is not good for you and I can't have you killing yourself because you let him get to you. I promise you this will work itself out."

Face took a deep breath but Revenge was set in those eyes. Tasha knew no matter what she said it wouldn't be over until he got back what was his and got his revenge. His eyes said everything and all she could do was pray that the love of her life would be in her life forever. She never wanted their time to run out but she always knew she was in love with a man who stood by his word…Face would have his revenge.

Washington, D.C…

C.W. Watson was incensed. Ever since the government had lost their major drug case against Face and his crime organization, he had been on his own personal mission to one day settle the score. He was embarrassed to look his staff and superiors in their eyes. He had failed them terribly by losing the biggest drug case in U.S. history. Now it was personal. He didn't want Face in a federal prison for the rest of his days, no he wanted blood. He wanted him dead along with Veronica, Pamela, Tasha and anyone else Face loved and cared for. As he sat back in his chair the knock on the door woke him up from his daydream.

"Hold on" he said, placing the oversized photos of Face, Veronica and Reese back inside his desk drawer. "Come on in" he said, as the door slowly opened and a short stocky, bald white man dressed in an all-black suit walked into the office. "Have a seat" Watson stated, and the man shook his hand before sitting.

The guest was Paul Warner, who is a man of many titles. Paul was a former Navy Lieutenant who had served in the Gulf War. He was now being used by the C.I.A., D.E.A. and the F.B.I. to do all of their dirty work; and often he was called in to clean up their messes. His nickname was the "Eraser" and people in high places feared him and knew he'd be better served as a friend than an enemy.

"So Paul what do you think?"

"I think it can be done. It will take some time, maybe a few years but if we plan everything well, in the next two to four years I will have Face and his whole organization exterminated from off the face of the earth. Just like that famous gangster rapper we had to get rid of. People still think the man is alive" Paul said, while a grin appeared upon his face.

"So two to four years, why so long?"

"Well sir, it will take some time to gather all the proper information we will need to dispose of this matter. There are a lot of players in this game. Plus you know Face is no small time catch, he's the biggest fish in the tank. This street hoodlum is actually quite intelligent and well-connected and protected. I have my people strategically placed around the East Coast, in Philly, New York, Jersey and in Baltimore gathering information on his personal life, his friends, his family, and any and everything they can dig up."

"Good because this man has humiliated me beyond words" C.W. Watson exclaimed, slamming his fist down on the desk.

"Do what you have to do. Just keep this quiet and clean up your mess when you're done. I don't care how many years it takes to erase him, just make sure you get rid of that bastard Face."

March 20th 2010
Three Years Later
West Philadelphia...

Inside a row-home on the 4200 block of Pennsgrove Street, Quincy and Doc had just walked upstairs after coming out of the basement; a pair of bloody surgical gloves were on Doc's hands.

"Thanks Doc, you always come in handy" Quincy said, as he walked over to the front door.

"No problem Quincy. Keep bringing them by, it keeps my juices flowing." Doc said, showing his devilish grin.

"Don't you worry Doc, Face has a lot of enemies, so you should be seeing plenty more, very soon."

"How is Face holding up…because I'm not sure if the rumors are true but I hear he got robbed for a billion dollars" Doc asked, trying to feed his curiosity.

Quincy giggled and nodded his head. He knew the streets were talking but ninety percent of the information that flows on Philly streets was incorrect.

"No Doc, ain't nobody get at him for a billion dollars. Don't believe everything you hear my man."

"Tell him to call me sometimes. I miss my friend. Tell him that I said he's not too big to come down to his old hood and visit ole Doc."

"Sure will" Quincy said, before walking out of the door.

Doc walked over to the curtains and watched as Quincy got inside of a dark blue Chevy Impala. After beeping the horn, Quincy pulled off down the street. Doc pulled the curtains shut and started walking towards the basement door. When he approached the door he heard a painful squeal coming from below. Doc closed the door behind him and made his way down the stairs. When he reached the bottom step he stopped and smiled. The sight of the nude white woman strapped to his lab table was the ultimate turn on.

The woman's eyes had been surgically removed and were lying inside of a glass pickle jar next to a long wooden·table. Blood ran down the sides of her face and she shivered uncontrollable; and not from the basement chill but from the sheer fear of what had happened to her and of what was to come.

Her name was Judy Powaski, the wife of Federal Agent Steve Powaski-who was one of many on a long list of Face's enemies. For two months Quincy had secretly been observing Judy and had her routine down to the minute. She was quite a simple woman and didn't deviate from the ritual of dropping the kids off, going to work, then to the gym, and on to picking up the children from daycare and then back home. He knew when he made his move it had to be a smooth and easy pick-up. He didn't want to be seen nor did he want to get into a scuffle, which would raise alarm and possible hinder his chances.

His moment came when she made a pit-stop at Starbucks on her way to work. The early morning was calm and the parking lot was empty. His face was barely visible with the ball cap he wore along with a neck scarf that was covering much of his face. He deliberately dropped some change to the ground, which landed under her car. When he went to retrieve the change from under the car, he quickly punctured her back tire and then gathered the change before getting back into his car.

When she walked out of the store carrying her Frappuccino with extra sugar, all seemed normal and she continued to move on with her daily routines. However, once on the road she began to hear a strange noise and pulled over on the side of the road to check it out. When she got out of the car her instincts told her something was wrong but she was sure it was nothing more than her nerves; since her husband had put the fear in her mind because he constantly warned her about getting out of the car when she was alone in isolated areas. Seeing that her tire was going flat, she knelled down and searched to see if she had run over a nail, or a bottle; which could have caused the flat tire. Then as she began to stand Quincy hovered over her and showed her a picture of her twin boys and her husband. He told her if she screamed or tried to cause a scene, he'd have them all killed. Filled with fear and uncertainty, she wasn't willing to risk the lives of her family so she got into the car with Quincy. Now she was in the hands of Doc and regretting each moment that she didn't put up a fight.

Doc walked over to his prey and he scanned her body and was delighted in her nudity. He leaned down to get his mouth close to her right ear and he said "I know you can't see me but you can hear me. We are going to have a lot of fun Judy, just you and I. Then, it's unfortunate, but you must die." He began to rub his bloody hands across her breast as if he was trying to console her, then he repeated "Then you must die."

Chapter 2
Later That Evening...

Detective Ron Perry pulled over and parked his unmarked police car at the corner of 52nd and Market Street. He puffed on his Newport long and waited patiently. As he blew a thick grey cloud of smoke into the misty air he noticed the heaps of traffic and people moving all around him. This location was one of the busiest intersections in West Philly. Hundreds of stores lined the streets and people from all over the city shopped the popular avenue for the best deals their money could buy.

Out the corner of his eye, Ron Perry spotted the young man he had been waiting for. As he began to walk towards his car he felt good to see him. It had been a while since they had last seen one another but the young man was a splitting image of his legendary father. Robbie got into the car and they gave each other a hug.

"Hey Uncle Ron," Robbie. said.

"Hey Jr., it's so good to see you. How is that beautiful sister of yours doing?"

"Arianna is doing fine. She's eighteen now and she goes to Temple University. She's going to be a lawyer one day."

"Wow, how time flies" Ron Perry said.

"Yeah, I know. I have to keep all the hawks and vultures away from her, she's too good for everybody. She's gonna hate how overprotected I am but I gotta protect my lil sis" Robbie said.

"Well, you gotta protect a diamond...ya know."

"Yeah."

Ron Perry started up his car and pulled off down the crowded street.

"So what's going on with you Jr.?"

"I'm good Uncle Ron, I'm just doing me."

"Doing you…what does that mean?"

"I realized that school just wasn't for me, so that's why I dropped out of Drexel. I have to peruse some other things that are a focal point for me."

"And what's that", Ron asked, as he turned onto Walnut Street.

"Revenge…I'm going to get revenge for my sister and me. I gotta get at all the people who had something to do with murdering my parents. I have money to make sure I get the things I need, and if anything happens to me I'll be okay; my concern now is only about Arianna. But she has money and she'll be set for life-my dad made sure of that. But nobodies trying to mess with me because of who my dad is. People still fear him and he's been dead for years."

"Why didn't you let me in on your plans?"

"Uncle, I know you want to help me but this is a personal matter. Face murdered my parents and I have to be the last face he sees before I end his life. I've been planning and rethinking exactly how I'm going to get him and now it's time for me to make good on the promise I made to my sister."

"So, you've been busy."

"Yeah, I know when I get him he's gonna wish he killed me when he had the chance."

"Listen, if you need me for anything don't hesitate to call me. I got connections and you know that I can make shit happen."

"I know, you'll be hearing from me soon."

They pulled up behind Robbie's 2010 all-white Mercedes S550, and before Robbie exited the car they shook hands. Ron Perry watched as Robbie got in his car and pulled off, and he smiled because he knew Face's time was limited.

19th & Erie
North Philly...

Inside an obscured stash house in North Philly, Face and Quincy were meeting to have a discussion. After the two shook hands the discussions begin.

"Thanks my brother. I'm really tired of playing this game of cat and mouse with people."

"I told you Face, I got your back always. As long as you need me I'm just a phone call away" Quincy said.

"Well, you'll be getting some more help in another week" Face said, as a grin formed on his face.

"I can't wait...I miss Reese and it will be good to see him again. That was my partner you know."

"Yup."

"Did he wise up or is that nigga still a loose cannon?"

"Both! When I talked to Reese it seems like he has grown but at times I can still hear the same ole Reese, but prison definitely changed him. He's humbled himself...but truth be told he needed a wake up call and I'm sure prison gave it to him" Face said, as he sat down in a black leather recliner chair.

"Did Doc take care of that problem for us?"

"Yup, I left the body with Doc so he could do his thing with her. Only the Lord knows what that will be", Quincy said, as the both begin laughing.

"Well I want them all dead…every last one of them and everyone they love! Agent McDonald, Agent Powaski, Truck, The Gomez brothers, and especially that crooked as detective, Ron Perry! I want him to pay for what he did to Momma and DJ, and I won't be fulfilled until he's eliminated" Face fumed.

Quincy saw the intensity in Face's eyes and just shook his head in agreement. Ron Perry would never be forgiven for taking Momma and DJ from him. They were good people and Ron was going to pay. Quincy turned his body towards Face, and he was now sitting in the identical recliner next to him and asked, "What about Peter?" Face stood up and strolled over to the grey steel front door to calm his nerves. The mention of Peter's name sent Face into a rage because he hadn't been able to get his hands on Peter. "Don't worry" Face said, "I have someone working on him and that pussy can't hide forever. He picked the wrong man to rob." Quincy was happy to hear something would be done to Peter. He knew the word on the street was that Face got got, and that could be a potential problem for a fool thinking they could test Face or his organization.

The two gathered themselves and headed for the door. Face walked Quincy to his car and shook hands with Kyle; he was a member of the team who had been hired tonight for security and often used to watch them as they met at this home. After Face said his goodbyes he got into his green Mercedes 600 SL and heading home. The soothing sounds of Maxwell flowed out of the Bose speakers and Face tried to let his racing thoughts subside. All he wanted was to go home and try to get a good night's sleep.

Agent Steve Powaski knew something was wrong. He could feel it every time he dialed his wife's cellular number. "Where the hell are you Judy" he said to himself. It wasn't like his wife not to answer his calls, and if she did miss he call she'd return the call within a few minutes or so. Suddenly his cell phone rang.

"Hello, Mr. Powaski."

"Yes, Mrs. Clark is there a problem" he asked, recognizing it was the daycare center.

"I'm not sure. The children haven't been picked up and I've been calling your wife but she hasn't answered."

"What…she didn't pick up the children."

"No and we have been closed for the past hour."

"I'm very sorry; I'll be there in a half an hour."

As he hung up there was an emptiness that filled his belly. Where was his wife? Why hadn't she picked up the phone? The questions that filled his mind made it hard for him to concentrate but he had to get the children.

Agent Powaski rushed to his car without delay. With his foot firmly pressed on the gas pedal, he sped off and said "Judy, where the hell are you?"

Fremont, Nebraska...

Encircled by miles and miles of open farmland, Vernon "Truck" Wilson stood out on his porch and stared at the greyish-blue sky. This was his routine and he would stare at the scenery for hours on end. Truck couldn't fully comprehend how drastic his life had changed. After giving his sworn testimony against Face during his federal trial, Truck had been placed in the Witness Protection Program.

His safety was surely at risk and enrolling in the program was the only way he could ensure he wouldn't get a bullet to the head. For four years he had been living in the small town of Fremont, using his newly government issued name, Jeffrey Lloyd. He was a lonely man because all contact with his family and friends had ended. They had no knowledge of his whereabouts and he knew how risky it would be to take a chance by contacting them.

As he breathed in the fresh, pure air, he thought about his life back in Philly. He smiled at the thoughts of making money, living the life of a Boss, and having sex with so many beautiful women that he had lost count. It was a life he missed dearly and one he wanted once more...but as the sounds of a flock of geese flying above brought him back to reality, he knew that Face would rather see him dead than to have him sit back on his throne.

Chapter 3
Graterford Prison...

Reese sat on his bunk playing an intense game of chess with his celly, Big Nas. This was the deciding game of their best out of five installments; and the score was currently tied-with each man having won two games. With a hundred dollar wager on the line, each player analytically scanned the board before making their moves; all the while hoping their opponent would make a crucial mistake.

"It's your move man" Reese said. Big Nas gave no verbal response; instead he nodded his head in agreement. After a few moments Big Nas moved his black bishop. Reese was pleased with the move and smiled as he reached for his white queen. "Checkmate" he exclaimed, because he had just trapped Big Nas' king with a queen-rook combination.

"Damn, I let your bum-ass beat me again" Big Nas said. "Let me...Nigga I be owning your big ass" Reese said, as he stood up from his bunk. Reese playfully got up in Big Nas' face to gloat. The towering six foot-five inches, two hundred pound man, whose body resembled a professional linebacker, laughed at Reese and playfully shoved him back. "Calm down Lil man...I let you win because you're going home real soon. Consider it a going home present." Reese laughed knowing he had just served Big Nas and said, "I'll take it."

Big Nas climbed up on his top bunk and got comfortable before finishing their conversation.

"Hey Reese..."

"Yeah, Nas wassup?"

"Don't forget me nigga when you get out of here" he said seriously.

"Come on homey I told you I got you. All a man got in this world is his word and his balls, and I don't break mind for nobody" Reese replied. "Alright..." Big Nas said, with uncertainty.

Reese stood up from his bunk and looked Big Nas sternly in his eyes and said, "I'm a hustler homey and more than that I'm a loyal ass dude. When you get out in another six months just make sure you get at me. I gave you all my contact and it ain't changing, so if you don't get at me then that's how you wanted it."

"No, I'm gonna call you for sure."

"Yeah man, I mean you held me down for almost four years up in this hell hole. We done fought together and rode together. That means a lot for-real. Face always told me that nothing in life is more important than a man's loyalty-Nothing!"

Reese reached his hand out to his friend and the two men shook hands and then Reese said, "Besides how can I forget the man I whopped in chess so often." They both started laughing as Big Nas set the chess board up for a rematch.

Early The Next Morning
Lincoln Drive...

A large group of F.B.I. agents all stood around the mutilated body of Judy Powaski. Her arms and feet had been dismembered and both eyes had been surgically removed. As the tears fell down the face of her husband, Agent Powaski, he reluctantly placed the crisp white sheet over her corpse. He didn't want to see his wife this way and at the same time he couldn't psychologically bring himself to accept the fact that she was actually lying dead in front of him. She would never tell him she loved him and the children would never be able to see their mother alive again. It was overwhelming and as the sheet lay on her body his mind turned to the perpetrator.

The forensic team had the area completely quarantined and were searching for any evidence and clues that would help them find the sick individual responsible for this heinous crime. While in thought he stood there, drifting in and out of consciousness. Agent McDonald came upon him and placed his arm around his longtime partner, before leading him away so the two could have some privacy.

"Don't worry Steve, we are going to find the son-of-a-bitch who is responsible for this and he'll pay for what he did to Judy, I promise that. Even if it takes the rest of my career and then some, we'll get that bastard and get our own justice." Steve listened as the words flew out of his partner's mouth but his mind was in another place. He was in shock and didn't understand it all. Why would anybody want to hurt his wife? She was a great mom, a lovely woman, and for the past fourteen years she had been his darling wife.

As the two men walked to their unmarked car, Agent McDonald continued to rant out his frustration. Little did he know that on the opposite side of town his wife, Tanya, had just been abducted by Quincy and she was now an unwilling passenger in the back of a tinted black van. Her mouth and hands were duct-taped and the driver was in route to Doc's place.

Later That Afternoon...

The all black, tinted Mercedes Benz pulled up and parked on the corner of 12th and Arch Streets. A short, heavyset, brown skinned woman nervously approached the car and got into the back seat. Face was comfortably seated there with a copy of the Philadelphia Daily News folded across his lap. He had a thick brown envelope in his hand and he passed it to the woman, who placed it into her pocketbook. "It's all there if you want to count it, and I put a little something extra in there."
"Oh, no need Mr. Face I trust you" the woman said.
"Karen, I really appreciate you getting me that information."
"Again, it was no problem and whenever you need me just let me know."
Face signaled his driver with the snap of his fingers and the car slowly pulled off down the street. As they reached 6th and Market, the car pulled over and Karen exited the car and walked away. Face was pleased and a grin graced his face. He then told his driver to move on as he picked up the Daily newspaper. The headline read: F.B.I. Agent's Wife Found Slain on Lincoln Drive.

After displaying her federal identification card, Karen Brown walked past the four-man security team and got on one of the empty elevators. As the elevator car ascended to the 7th floor she tried her best to appear composed and oblivious. When the doors opened she hurried to her desk, which was located in the main lobby, but she was stopped just before taking her seat by a female co-worker.

"Oh my god Karen, did you hear the terrible news about Agent Powaski's wife?" She did her best to seem sympathetic and replied, "Yes I did...I just heard. This world is so cruel I swear. I just hope they find whoever did this" Karen said, as she began to log into her computer. "Me too" her co-worker Nancy said, before shaking her head in disgust and walking away.

Karen Brown had been employed with the federal government for over eight years. She was one of the handful of secretaries that had complete access to the private files of government employees. With just a tap of her computer key she could bring up personal information on all the employees who worked in her bureau.

Just six months prior she had met Quincy in a crowded bar down in Northern Liberties. The two talked and exchanged numbers in what seemed like a chance meeting. Within a few weeks she was having the best sex of her life. She had never climaxed as hard and as frequent with any man, and Karen was sprung-to the point nothing was off limits with

Quincy; not even the government's classified information. She could tell how pleased Quincy was when she talked about her job and how much information she could provide him, so she let out all she knew and promised to find out more and more.

Quincy used his scouting skills to trap her. Face knew they needed a mole inside of the bureau and Quincy had someone else in mind, but luckily stumbled upon Karen. She was one of the least attractive and the most unnoticeable women in Philadelphia; but once she nearly knocked him over as he was going to pull the metro out of the newspaper dispenser, he noticed her work badge and knew she could possibly supply him with heaps of priceless information.

Quincy made Karen feel as if she was the most beautiful women on this earth and in return she bowed to him like a king. She was his puppet and he was her puppet-master. Karen was in love and had no clue she was selected for a covert mission. Before meeting Quincy her life was filed with trips to the library, lonely dinners, and long conversations with her cat; but now everything had changed. There was a spark in her life now and someone finally knocked the cobwebs off of her aging pussy. Not to mention she was enjoying the pay, considering the thick brown envelope held ten thousand dollars in compensation.

As she began typing on her computer she had no concern for the murder that had taken place. She was tired of living in the shadows of life and was happy to have a man and some extra money to spruce up her physical appearance. As she browsed the internet for a spa so she could get a body wax and checked out Victoria Secret for a new bra and panty set, she thought to herself, "Oh how I love my new life."

Chapter 4
King of Prussia Mall

The mall was packed with shoppers. The weekends were always the busiest days for the well-known shopping center. After a few hours in Nordstrom's, Pamela and Veronica exited the mall with their bags filled with designer dresses and shoes, before making their way to the car. Veronica pressed her key-pad for the automatic trunk opener on her all white Bimmer. They placed their bags in the trunk and Veronica hurried to the driver's seat, and then pressed the button again for the trunk to close.

"Why are you in a rush" Pamela asked. "Oh, I have a meeting with a new client and I want to make a good first impression" Veronica said with a smile, as she pulled out of the parking spot. "Oh, I thought you were retired." Pamela said, looking at her girlfriend for some truth. "I was. I mean I have been for the last year and half...but I decided to come back. The money is too good and the excitement is even better."

Pamela looked at Veronica whose eyes looked like she was remembering all the good times, and said "Just remember what Face said. The Feds won't ever give up until they have us all locked up in cages. You have to be careful." Veronica looked at Pam while they were stopped at the red light and said, "Fuck the Feds! Fuck them all!"

Pamela knew Veronica was always cautious but she needed to tell her friend to stay on alert. She knew neither of them wanted to be sitting in a cell and getting weekly visits, so they had to keep their eyes open and their hands clean. For now Pamela would listen to the excitement that this new client brought.

"So who is this new friend of yours?"

"He's a business man from New York City."

"Business man, what business is he in to?"

"He's legit; a good friend of mine referred him to me. He's a stock broker on Wall-street. One of those lame asses with a whole lot of money, that will do most anything I say."

As they drove on the earlier warnings about the Feds now had Veronica a bit spooked. She started to think it was some truth to the warning so she asked, "Do you really think they are still watching us? It's been over three years since Face beat that case." Pamela got serious and replied, "Yes, they are. Face said they'd watch us for the next ten years if they felt they could take him and all of us down. That's why we have to stay focused and five steps ahead of all Face's enemies and our own. I'm sure you're on somebody's hit list girl." Veronica looked at Pam and said, "I did get him acquitted... not to mention those secret tapes are what freed him."

Veronica paused and thought to herself about the true danger she could be in. She had to be extra cautious about anyone new she invited in to her life, or even associated with. She turned to Pamela and said, "Girl I'm going to be careful for sure, but don't worry about my new friend. Like I said, he's just a lame with some money that will soon become my money." Veronica began driving on the expressway and Pamela said, "Just make sure we keep those tapes safe and we'll always have an edge on those jokers.

Those are our lifesavers and our get out of jail free cards!" They both laughed as the newly waxed car shined as it sped off.

Chapter 5
Later That Night...

As darkness fell on the city of Philadelphia, only a few stars filled the calm skies; and as Doc walked to a deserted area of Fairmount Park not even his lax footsteps could be heard. With his small flashlight in one hand and his large suitcase in another, Doc had found the perfect spot to dispose of his newest victim.

Doc hands were covered by his black, leather gloves, and as he got down on his knees he could hear the distant sounds of crickets and saw one lone squirrel looking for nuts. Doc began to brush away the falling leaves from the spot he kneeled upon before opening the large suitcase. Inside was the mutilated body of Tanya McDonald. Her head, feet, and hands had been surgically cut away from her body; and just like her deceased girlfriend Judy, her eyes were also in the refrigerator inside of Doc's pickle jar.

Doc was careful as he laid Tanya's head on the ground, and then he placed her hands and feet beside it. He stared at the pieces like a proud sculptor or painter, before closing the suitcase and calmly walking away. After just a few steps he stopped and turned back to his victim and said, "I'm sorry for what I've done to you and so many others...but my friend Face is very upset with his enemies. Too bad your husband happened to be one of them." He started to walk away but said "Oh, I almost forgot, sleep well beautiful", before walking off.

Forty Minutes Later...

When Doc returned home he took off all his clothes and sneakers, before burning them- along with the large suitcase in an oversized metal trashcan in his backyard. He knew he couldn't leave any evidence around. He was careful to bleach down anything his victims came in contact with, as well as getting rid of any hair or skin particles. He was meticulous and precise when it came to cleaning up any messes. Doc even went as far as to shaving off all the hair on his head and his body; the only hair he had left was on his eyebrows. He looked like a shorter version of Uncle Fester from the Adams Family, and he was just as creepy.

Once he was done he took a long hot shower. He put on his plush black robe and went downstairs to get the pickle jar out of the refrigerator. Doc walked over to his couch and picked up the remote control from his coffee table, before sitting down. He scanned through the stations before he came across his favorite show CSI.

As he relaxed and enjoyed the suspenseful plots and the detective work of the forensic scientist; he opened the small pickle jar and took out one of the eyeballs. He knew it was his job to get rid of the evidence, so he opened his mouth and swallowed it whole.

As he licked his lips, enjoying the after taste and texture of his late night treats, he took another eyeball from the pickle jar. There were three things Doc enjoyed in life; killing people, being a loyal friend to Face, and the delectable taste of human eyes.

Villanova, PA...

Face laid across his large plush king size bed, enjoying the relaxing and soothing feel of Tasha's soft hands. She knew his mind was full and she wanted to help ease some of the tension he was overloaded with. Tasha was the one woman who could relax him. She was his soul mate and his rock. With her he could trust her with his life and the bond they shared was inseparable.

As she continued to caress her man she saw he was still uneasy, so she asked,
"What are you thinking about my love?"
"Business, Reese coming home, enemies, and the list goes on and on."
"Well our businesses are doing great, I told you that. We really are doing good. This quarter our profits increased by twenty percent. As far as Reese is concerned, he'll be fine...he has you."
"It's my enemies that are getting under my skin. I just can't seem to eliminate them fast enough and before I know it here comes a new batch of them. I want them all gone now."
"You have to be patient and wait to the time is right. You've been handling that aspect of your life and nothing has to change. You know what you need to do" she said, as she leaned over and stroked the scar on his face.

Face turned around on his back and looked into Tasha's deep brown eyes. For a moment they stared into each other's eyes before Face said "I'm going to get them all. No one will get close to me or my family." Tasha leaned in and kissed him softly before saying, "Baby, every one of your enemies is my enemy. They are enemies to our children, our family and our friends. Do what you have to but please promise one thing..." Face looked at his wife and said, "Whatever you want, just name it." She looked at him because she knew he might be making a promise he couldn't keep if he allowed his anger and hatred to conquer his mind. "Face, I need you to come home to us. I need you to make it back here because Lil Norman and Suri need their father around, and I'm nothing without my better half. I need you to do that every night."

The tears had begun to fall down Tasha's face because the thought of losing her husband was a thought she never wanted to be a reality. She knew the life he lived had been filed with corruption, violence, and that many people envied him and wanted his power and wealth; but still she could never come to terms with Face being taken away from her and their children.

As Face placed his arms around her, he pulled Tasha closer and said "I promise, I ain't goin nowhere." He lay her down on the bed and begin to slowly remove her underwear until he had her completely naked. Then he began to kiss, suck, and slurp on her clitoris, and as her liquids amplified she began to relax and enjoy the pleasures the night was surely to bring.

Chapter 6

Inside of her elegant home, Veronica and her new male lover laid their naked bodies across her oversized bed. For hours the two had had been locked in a world of sexual bliss and had just taken a break.

"Veronica, your body is simply amazing."

"Thank you Carter, yours isn't bad either."

"So tell me something Cater. Why doesn't a rich, educated, well hung, handsome, and did I say rich man, like yourself have a wife?"

"Would it matter if I did have a wife?"

"Nope, we are here on business and just because it's filled with pleasure doesn't meant that it's any less business."

"Good answer baby. I knew you were professional."

Veronica didn't care if he was married, gay, or even a cross-dresser but she always dug to see what information she could get from her clients. Veronica was a skilled professional and had slept with women and men, with all types of stories and backgrounds. For her sex could never be anything more than a business. At the end of the day she wanted money and never got caught up with her clients. It was a life of fantasy and cash and when the doors closed, the fantasy ended and the money was paid.

As they continued to lie across the bed Carter heard the vibrations from his cell phone. He reached for his pants and pulled his blackberry out of his pockets. When he saw the name on the caller id, he asked Veronica to excuse him as he got up to take the call. She suggested he take the call in front of her because she told him she'd keep quiet, but he insisted he take it in private.

The caller had hung up by the time he had gotten off the bed and was ready to head out of the bedroom into the living room. Veronica got up and made her way to the kitchen to get some water and Carter hurried into the living room, as the phone began to ring again. Veronica had slept with enough married men to know when a guys' wife was calling. She smiled because she knew that information could always be valuable.

Early The Next Morning...

The F.B.I. office was in total chaos. In just two days the wives of two of their top agents had been murdered and their bodies were mutilated. An all-out manhunt had been issued for the person or persons responsible for the kidnapping and murders of Judy Powaski and Tanya McDonald. Hundreds of cops and agents were searching the streets of Philadelphia for any evidence they could get their hands on. The F.B.I. also put up a reward of $200,000 for any information leading to the arrest of the killer or killers.

The phones were ringing off the hook and informants were looking and even creating tips in hopes of cashing in on the reward. These crimes were a big deal and they had no true starting point. The wives had no known enemies but this seemed to be a targeted hit; and although their husbands worked in the bureau there were no recent incidents that would have marked them as targets either.

For the F.B.I. this was not only a horrific blow but also an embarrassment to the agency. One of the most sophisticated law enforcement agencies was now clueless and had no idea where to start looking for the killers; and they weren't' sure that the killer wasn't going to strike again.

International Airport
Washington, D.C...

For over three years Peter J Greenberg had been traveling around the world spending Face's money. He had visited many of the countries in Europe, Africa and Asia. He was spending Face's money as if it was growing and falling off of trees. With hundreds of millions at his disposal he was like a kid in a candy store. Peter was living the life he had always wanted but the only problem was it wasn't his money that had afforded him his current lifestyle.

As he sat in his private jet, he looked out of the window and he knew it was only minutes that separated him from touching the soil that could end all his good fortune. The sight of the U.S. made him remember the day he left. He had expected Face to lose at trial and he'd get away scot-free. Never did he think Face stood a chance at being a free-man once he went into that courtroom. Peter had been running ever since that day because he knew he had robbed the biggest drug dealer in U.S. history for 500 million dollars. There was a bounty on his head and he was not safe back in the United States.

Now he was back to talk to the U.S. Government. They had located him in Dubai with three beautiful women, and gave him 72 hours to return. Peter knew that if the government could track him down he had no choice but to jump on his deluxe Beechcraft Premiere 1 Jet and head to Washington, D.C. The only other problem he had now was worrying about who else knew he was coming back to America.

Chapter 7

Ron Perry walked out of the 33rd district police precinct and got inside of his unmarked police car. Although most officers felt these cars were incognito most street criminals could recognize these cars a mile away. As he drove off he bought a Philadelphia Daily News from a local street vendor. The headline read: *F.B.I. Still Clueless over Dead Wives*. He paused and said "It's Face you damn idiots!" He knew no one else had the power and connections to have the women placed under surveillance, and then kidnapped and murdered.

Ron was fuming. Why didn't these damn fools put the pieces together and get this asshole off the streets he thought. The veins on the left side of his face were pulsating as he continued to wonder why Face wasn't being brought in for questioning. He shouted out "Why didn't you damn fools let me take that shot! He would have been dead by now." A woman in a car that was passing by looked at him like he was crazy because he was having a full blown conversation, but he was the only one in his car.

The frustration and anger he felt came from his gut feelings that Face had killed Hood and his wife. Ron hated Face and no matter how long it took he'd pay him back for what he did; and he not only wanted Face but Reese, who he knew played a major role in the murders as well.

Face sat inside of the spacious Mercedes Benz in a trance. As his driver drove around Philly his mind was in a thousand places. A man who desperately wanted to get his mind back on track was unable to because no matter what his priorities were, not matter how committed he was to his family, the distractions were always making their way into his mind and throwing him off track. At times he would muster up a smile when he thought about his family but that would quickly fade away as the thought of Peter came his way. Peter had taken from him what was promised for his family. He had made their way out and wanted them to be a powerful family for many years to come. Without the bulk of his wealth he felt like a man with boxers on; simply no security net. He was a brief wearing type of guy, and he needed to feel secure at all times.

As the driver pulled on to I-95, his IPhone rung. He looked at the caller's name and a huge grin came across his face.

"Hello my good friend."

"Face, are you ready for me now?"

"In a few more days I will be. That's when my partner gets out of prison."

"Okay, that's fine. I'll be looking forward to meeting him. Any friend of yours is a friend of mine" the man said, with a Latin accent.

"Did you find out anything about the brothers?"

"Yes, I have all the info you need to settle the score. You know I hate snitches, especially the ones that allow the government to convince them to turn on their brothers."

"Thanks Roberto, I really need that info and it

couldn't have come at a better time."

"You got it my good friend. I'm looking forward to working with you for a very long time. Men like you Face are hard to find in this business of ours. Nowadays a stand up man is a true find and a blessing once you have one on your team."

"I really appreciate that Roberto; I will see you in a few days."

"Cool, adios" he said, and the call ended.

Bogota, Columbia...

Roberto Fuentes stood on the porch of his vast, off-white mansion. Surrounded by six armed guards, he inhaled the cool Columbian air and watched as the birds freely flew over his luxurious home. Roberto Fuentes was the leader of the Los Rastrojos group; an organization that is currently engaged in the Columbian armed conflict. This Cartel is considered to be the largest supplier of drugs in Columbia, and they collaborate with a wide range of Mexican syndicates; including the most powerful Sinaloa Cartel.

Roberto Fuentes is a man of great power and wealth. He's one of the most powerful men on earth who specializes in the worldwide transportation of cocaine, heroin, and marijuana. This tall dark man, who graduated from Yale University, was not only influential but he was educated and fluent in French, Spanish, Japanese and Arabic. He had been on the government's radar for a few years but so far he remained untouchable.

After reading up on Face's drug trial a few years earlier, he had waited for the perfect opportunity to reach out to him. The initial meeting left both men impressed with each other's character and they kept in contact through phones which were untraceable and couldn't be hacked by any government devices. Both men saw there was a need for each other. Roberto needed a trustworthy distributor in the states and Face needed another powerhouse connect to get his wealth back to where it belonged.

No matter how many times Face looked at his bank statements and his stash, no amount of money would set him straight until he got back what Peter took and then some. Many men can never imagine making a million dollars in their lifetimes but Face was not just any man. He had dreamt of one day being a multi-billion dollar man and he knew there was no reason why he couldn't make his dreams come true. He had started from the bottom and made moves that no one he had come up with had made. He was a self-made man and now he was back on his grind, but this time he was going harder.

Roberto and Face also shared a common enemy in the Gomez brothers. Face hated them because they testified against him and Roberto despised them for disrespecting their roots and snitching. The code didn't change just because one crossed waters, snitching was deplorable on all sides of the sea. Roberto watched the entire trial on CNN and was furious to see the two brothers spilling their guts live on the airways. Roberto Fuentes was a proud, dignified man, and loyalty was a priority with him. Anyone who didn't live by the same code of ethics as him was an enemy; and seeing how the Gomez brothers were not men of merit-they were currently added to his hit-list.

Chapter 8
The Crowne Plaza Hotel
City Line Avenue...

Inside of a private suite on the 6th floor of the Crowne Plaza hotel, the sounds of avid, heat-filled moans could be heard coming down the hallway. Quincy had Karen bent over the bed with her legs spread wide apart, and his hands were firmly placed on her thick thighs as he aggressively fucked her from behind. Between strokes he'd ask "Whose pussy is this" and she was so turned-on she could fill herself about to be overtaken by her climax. As she was compelled to scream, she shouted out "Yours Daddy" and this only made Quincy give it to her harder.

Karen was not a beautiful women and surely not one that Quincy would have wanted to fuck, so it was hard for him to do anything with her pussy but to beat it up. She was so wet and he didn't understand how she could be turned all the way up with the way he treated her. He didn't caress her, kiss her, suck her titties or even eat her pussy, but she would deep throat him, swallow his cum and she was even willing to eat his ass if that was what he wanted.

As Quincy felt the urge to cum, he started to fuck Karen harder and harder. Tears begin to form in her eyes and she could feel a sensation vibrating from her spine down to her feet. Quincy too felt her cuming and as he jammed his dick in her harder and deeper, the two burst at the same time. When he pulled out, Karen began having multiple orgasms and she begin to squirt all over the room. She lay back on the bed trembling and in a state of nirvana. Quincy was all she wanted and there was nothing she wouldn't do to make him happy.

South Philadelphia...

Agents McDonald and Powaski sat inside of their black Ford Taurus with solemn expressions upon their faces. They couldn't understand why their lives had been destroyed and furthermore had not yet come to a conclusive fact of who had murdered their wives. It would have been one thing if the women had been in a tragic car or plane accident but for both of the women to be kidnapped and dismembered, there was a gaping hole driven in their hearts that would never be repaired.

Each day after the horrendous events, the agents were tirelessly working the streets and searching for answers but they were falling hard on their luck. There was no evidence at the scenes, not even a strand of hair or a shoe or boot print. They knew they had to be dealing with a killer of higher intelligence but still they were sure they'd catch him; even though at times they had moments of doubts.

"I can't go on like this" McDonald, said as he allowed himself to let a few tears fall down onto the pants of his black suit. Powaski did what he could to offer support by placing his hands on his shoulder and saying, "We will get them man, just don't give up and stay focused. Something will come up soon. We always have cases where someone slips up or someone wants a way out of their own shit and drops us a line or two about someone else. Just stay with

me and we'll nail that son-of-a-bitch to the cross."
McDonald relished in the thoughts of killing the man
who slaughtered his wife and took his best friend
from him. He knew that if the killer wasn't found
soon nothing good would become of him.

These two man shared a hurt that none would
ever want to feel. Powaski had been with his wife for
over nineteen years and she was his one and only
love. They met in college and he knew that she'd be
the only women he'd ever give his heart too. He hurt
so deeply that it burnt. At times he could feel the
flames of anger and pain rising from his flesh and
there was nothing he could do to extinguish his
agony. Both men understood that they would not get
a moments rest until they put the killer to sleep-
permanently…but who in the hell were they looking
for?

15th & Diamond Street
North Philly…

Robbie watched as his beautiful younger
sister, Arianna, walked towards his car. She had just
finished her final class of the day and he came to pick
her up. The two embraced with a hug and he gave her
a kiss on the cheek. Since their parents were
murdered the two had been inseparable. Both lived
together. They shared a luxurious two bedroom
condominium in the Center-city section of
Philadelphia.

Lately, during the day while Arianna was in
school, Robbie would ride around trying to gather
information on his brother Face. Most times he'd run

into a dead end and other times he'd get pieces of information that didn't lead up to what he was looking for.

Robbie was starting to feel as if Face was untouchable. People who said they knew him would have a different story of who he really was, and never knew exactly how to get in contact with him. Robbie was growing frustrated and felt as if his brother had achieved some type of legendary status, but to him Face was nothing but a coward who had killed his parents.

Robbie kept every news article that had been written on his brother. He watched the street DVD's that were done on Face and watched rap videos where rappers would pay homage to him. He was a hero to so many and Robbie never forgot about the good times they shared when they were younger, because Face had been kind and loving to him.

As they were about to pull off, he saw woman who reminded him of his mother, and he instantly began to relive one of his painful childhood memories.

1989
Twenty Years Earlier
Los Angeles, CA...

"Come here Lil Robbie, come play with your big-brother." Robbie grabbed his bottle of milk and crawled towards his older brother Face. It was amazing and always a pleasure for Face to watch his young brother connect with him. He was only an infant but the bond the two of them shared was strong, and surely stronger than the bond Lil Robbie had for his own mother Pamela.

Face and Lil Robbie sat on the floor playing with oversized wrestling action figures, and Lil Robbie was fascinated with the bright yellow costume of Hulk Hogan. Just like most children, Lil Robbie would put the toy in his mouth, drool all over it, and throw it, but then cry for the toy as soon as Face picked it up.

Suddenly the door of the bedroom swung open and Pamela stood there with a distasteful look upon her face. "Face, hurry up and put on your shoes so I can take you to the playground." Face was excited and looked under the bed and got his shoes but then he turned to his mother and said, "Oh mom, what about Lil Robbie? Should I get his jacket and shoes too?" Pamela shot Face a looked as if that question didn't even deserve and answer, and said "No, don't worry about him. Your Uncle Allen will watch him...now hurry up."

Face wasn't one to give up on spending time with his brother, especially since he liked to see Lil Robbie smile and giggle on the swings. So he begged his mom until she eventually gave in. You could tell she wasn't happy about her decision to bring Lil Robbie but she wanted to keep her loving son Face pleased.

15th & Diamond Street
North Philly...

Arianna tapped Robbie because he had been sitting in a daze. A women motorist started blowing her horns at him because she wanted to know if she could get his parking spot. Robbie was stunned at how misplaced he had just gotten. The memories of his past were powerful and he didn't think they would stop until he settled the score. He had no love for his mother but there had been some emotional connection to Face. How could he ever forget how Face came to his rescue so many times? But more importantly Robbie knew that inside of him flowed the pure blood of Hood... and he was always going to be Hood Jr. and that is where his loyalty would lie.

Chapter 9
F.B.I. Headquarters
Washington, DC...

Led by two F.B.I. agents, Peter J. Greenberg walked down the long corridor and they stopped when they reached the last door on the right. Nervousness swept through his trembling body and he had no notion of what the U.S. Government wanted with him. For them to track him down in Dubai and demand his return to the states this had to be serious; but exactly how severe was this matter?

When he entered into the room there were already two men seated at the long round table. Each man had a stern look upon his face and gave off the impression there would be no good-cop/bad-cop games played today. Peter knew that the Feds were serious and they didn't come calling unless they had something serious to discuss.

"Have a seat Peter" Paul Warner said, and Peter who was now noticeably frightened did as he was told. "Fellas thanks a lot, you can wait outside until were done" Paul said. After the two men exited the room, Paul looked at the other man at the table and waited for him to speak.

"Peter how are you?"

"Not too well..."

"I understand, well my name is C.W. Watson and I'm the head of the Anti-Drug Commission. I like to get straight to the point, is that okay."

"Yes sir."

"Great, well we know everything about you Mr. Greenberg. All the scams you've been running on Wall Street, as well as your connections to some major drug traffickers."

Peter nodded his head and didn't utter a word. So far the information he was provided with was true but still he felt nothing was said that would implicate him in any crime. If they had any direct information on his Wall Street scams, they'd have to outright show it; and as far as whom he associated with he saw no crime in that.

"We know all about the businesses you own. The corporate Jet Company in Miami, the ten different dealerships throughout the U.S., and you have a major connection with the Ukrainian-born crime boss Semion Mogilevich. I'm sure you know he's the leader of the Russian mob."

Again Peter nodded not wanting to say anything. "We know that you are a very wealthy man and that you are very well on your way to being one of the top 10 richest men in the world."

Paul stood up from the table and walked over to Peter. He had grown tired of the head-nods and wanted to hear what Peter had to say. "You're a thief. You're one of the biggest thieves in U.S. history" he barked. Watson opened up a folder that had been sitting on the table in front of Peter.

Peter knew the evidence was a glance away. He had been skeptical of a possible positive outcome but now he was starting to feel he was not coming out of this room unscathed. Watson began to run down the facts. "In 1987 you stole thirteen million from Warren Buffet, in 1988 you stole 20 million from Donald Trump and I guess you were feeling lucky because you got Bill Gates for a measly 16 million.

You've stolen money from all your local executives and even gotten money from your foreign partners in China. Oh, and the money you invested with the Genovese Crime family, we know that you stole that back from them too. But wait, I don't want you to speak yet because there's more…You've also robbed the largest Japanese crime syndicate, the Yakuza. Oh, and your latest victim, Norman "Face" Smith Jr.; do you remember him? You managed to ruffle his feathers when you stole roughly 500 million from him. I think he is really pissed with you Peter", Paul said as he slowly shook his head.

Peter was no more good. He had been exposed for the crook he was. He knew a long time ago he should have left his criminal activities alone but he was addicted to the thrill. He didn't need money, he had plenty of it but the thrill kept him engaged in such a risky business. He knew that anyone of his victims could have gotten him killed but the mention of Face's name made the possibility seem as if someone would be picking out his casket shortly.

"You are a wanted man Peter. Your head is wanted all around the world but I think you know Face doesn't let things like this slide." Peter was scared and he wanted protection from Face. He knew it was time to pay the piper. "What do I have to do", Peter asked. Watson smiled and said, "We need all you have on Face and I do mean all of it. You were responsible for his money, so you know where it came from and where it went. We want to know about all of his shareholdings, his homes, and any secret accounts that you set up for him."

Peter felt drained and he hadn't even begun to spill he guts. He had been confronted with undisputable facts but true to his character he asked the one question that any stern, strewed, cut-throat business man would. "What do I get out of all this?" Paul reached out and grabbed Peter by the collar and said "You get to keep your life and if you don't help us, I'll deliver you to Face personally."

There was no other decision for him to make. Peter stood to lose not only his life but his multi-billion dollar empire. He thought it was a good deal but wanted to ensure his money was safe. "And the money" he slowly uttered, and Watson said, "Your money is yours but Face is ours." Peter was relieved to hear that he would still be able to keep his fortune. Just then Watson turned to him and said, "Oh, I almost forget…you will be under twenty-four hour surveillance at the Hilton, with a private detail until this case is finalized." Peter was beginning to feel a whole lot better and then Paul said, "Yes, we've got you covered and it will only set you back a billion dollars."

Peter became angry. He was being swindled by the government and there was nothing he could do about it. The scared man who had entered the room afraid and timid, was now seeing red because what mattered most to him was about to be taken away. His life work was stealing money and acquiring wealth, and now he was going to feel what it was like to be robbed. Peter knew the government played dirty but he wasn't ready to lie down and be their bitch.

"I think I'll take my chances and just do my own thing." Watson laughed and almost chocked on the water he had just began to drink. "This is no democracy Peter; you will never walk out of this room on your terms. If you want to leave this room you will be entering a cell that you'll probably die in. We have more than enough evidence to get you a life sentence. So to clear things up I'll tell you exactly what's about to transpire. In less than forty-eight hours you will give us access to your two off-shore accounts. We will remove 500 million from each account and then we'll turn back over access to you. Afterwards if you want to change the passwords for a little added security, go on ahead. We fully understand the need of updating and changing passcodes frequently. It's usually recommended that you do that about every three to six months, but in this case…well you get me don't you."

Tears were in the corners of Peter's eyes and he was doing all he could to keep them from falling out. He was getting raped but no one was actually penetrating him; and he couldn't put up a fight. "So I'm being robbed? What the fuck! You act like you wanted Face but you're coming after me!" Watson and Paul laughed at his outburst. Watson face became stern and he said "I'm here to get both of you fools. That son-of-a-bitch embarrassed me and my reputation is on the line; and you, you stupid fuck. Did you think you would live the rest of your life on the beaches of Maui? You're sloppy and cocky and your type always ends up on the other side. We may have taken a little longer to bring you in but you've always been on my list."

Peter put his head down on the table. He was going to do what they wanted and get his money back one day. He had an Arabian investor in Dubai who was tied to the distribution of oil, and well let's just say Peter was not going to let anyone take a billion dollars from him without having a plan to get it back.

As the meeting came to a close Paul called for the two men who would escort the party to the private suite in the Hilton Hotel. As all five men left the F.B.I. headquarters and entered the all black SUV, a pair of spying eyes was surprised to see Peter J. Greenberg. He had been searching with a watchful eye for the past three years and finally he had seen his target.

When the SUV pulled off he followed but stayed within an appropriate distance so that he was not noticed. While tailing the men he picked up his cell phone and placed a call.

"Face, I found Peter."

"What, are you sure?"

"Yes, he's riding in a car with Watson and some other officials."

"No bullshit."

"Man, I got photos and all, check your email. They just left the federal building and I'm tailing them now."

"Mike, you've made my day man. Thanks."

"This is what I get paid to do."

"Keep a close eye on them, I can't risk losing that motherfucker."

"No, ain't nothing getting lost over here. I'm on it."

"Alright, I'll be in touch soon."

Mike Conway was one of the best private investigators on the East Coast. He came highly recommended and even though he was expensive to employ, he guaranteed his ability to produce. He was a former military intelligence officer who had served several tours in Iraq and Afghanistan. He had been given an honorable discharge because his left wrist was shattered and he suffered 2nd degree burns on most of the bottom-half of his body when his division was ambushed by enemy fire. Now he was using his talents to fund the life he always wanted. His clientele was distinguished and the benefits allowed him to travel the world, dine at the finest restaurants, purchase the latest intelligence equipment, and have his way with the ladies.

Mount Erie Section of Philadelphia...

Inside of the corner brick home, Face and Quincy were sitting at a long cherry oak kitchen table in front of a MacBook Pro. The video and pictures were indubitably of Peter J. Greenberg. As Face watched the video he was filled with delight and anticipation. "This dude didn't even try to disguise himself though" Quincy said, looking at Face to get his thoughts. "Right. I'm confused why he thought he could walk around so loosely when I got a fucking bounty on his head...but it's cool. I'm going to dress him up real nice." Quincy knew what Face meant and was ready for the word.

"I'm going to need you and a few of our men up in DC. I want Peter back in Philadelphia" he said, as Quincy erupted in laughter. "What the fuck is up with you. Philadelphia though...you on your business-suit shit right now." Face, laughed because he knew sometimes he'd get intense but he knew what the men had lined up was no laughing matter. He knew the detail guarding Peter would have to be wiped out, along with anyone else who stood in the way. Peter J. Greenberg would be brought back to Face. But right now he was filled with a good feeling so he smiled. "I want him back in Philly, you good with that Quincy" he said, as Face looked at Quincy and the two shook hands and then exited the home.

Chapter 10
One Week Later
Graterford Prison...

The heavily tinted black Mercedes Benz limousine pulled up and parked in the prison parking lot. Moments later Reese, who was escorted to the front gate by two armed guards, appeared wearing his blue prions uniform and carrying a small bag filled with his personal belongings. Waiting inside of the limo was Face, Quincy, Pamela, Tasha, Passion-who was Reese's wife- and their four year old daughter Amaya.

Once Reese entered the limo everyone began celebrating. He tried to make his way to a seat but his daughter jumped into his arm and screamed "Daddy I love you and I can touch you now." It was the innocence and truthfulness of his daughter that melted his heart and brought him to tears. Reese quickly wiped his face and hugged his daughter and told her, "I love you baby."

Quincy popped a bottle of champagne and passed everyone a glass. Little Amaya was even given a glass but she was poured sparkling apple-cider.

"Four long years and my man is back home with his family. We stood beside you and not a day passed when you weren't in our thoughts. We love you, we're glad your back to stay and as always the future is ours" Face said, raising his glass and everyone said cheers before drinking their champagne.

As the celebration continued and the limo sped on, no one paid attention to the tinted blue ford

Taurus that cautiously followed them. Inside of the car were two F.B.I. field agents who had been given strict orders by Paul Warner to follow the moves of the newly released man. Paul knew he would be right under Face's wing and Paul's newest assignment was to bring down Norman "Face" Smith Jr.

Two Days Later
Fremont, Nebraska...

Truck walked into the local F.B.I. office and demanded to speak with the man in charge. The thin, white, elder and pleasant secretary told him to take a seat in the lobby and wait until his name was called. After about fifteen minutes the secretary led him to an office. She knocked on the wooden door, before opening it and ushering Truck in through the door.

"I want to leave this program" Truck yelled to the white heavyset man who sat at his desk. "Mr. Wilson, have a seat and let's talk about this" Mr. Lacey said. "I don't need a seat; I need to get the hell out of the program. I have to get back home so I can be myself. I feel locked up out here." Mr. Lacey got up from his seat and walked over to Truck. "You can't be serious" he said, as he placed his arm on Truck's shoulder, "You won't be able to survive without our help."

Truck shrugged his hand from his shoulder and said "I don't want to hide anymore. I'm out here with no family, no friends, nothing. This shit is driving me crazy...I'm better off home. I had more damn freedom in prison than I have out here. I want out man, I want out." Mr. Lacey was very confused.

He couldn't understand why anyone would want to put their life at risk but he knew it was not mandatory to keep someone in the program. If you wanted out, then they would let you walk.

Mr. Lacey walked over to his file cabinet and pulled out Truck's file. "Mr. Wilson are you sure you want out? I have to make it clear to you that people who leave the program have been killed, and you're no different than those people. We are here to protect you and keep you alive." Truck was ready to get out; he said "I'll take my chances." Mr. Lacey pulled out the release papers and without hesitation Truck grabbed a pen off of the desk and signed all five pages.

In that moment he felt alive. He was Truck again and never wanted to be anything else but that. He had been living the last few years of his life in fear and wanted to live the rest of his life as a free man. He knew what he had done. He had snitched, he was labeled a rat, and he knew that the demons of his past might catch up with him in the future but as he stood in the present he didn't give a fuck.

As he made his way to the front door, he smiled as he looked at his Escalade Truck that was parked out front. He had all his belongings inside and as he made his way back to his true home in Philly, he knew he was going back for better or for worse.

Washington, D.C...

Private investigator, Mike Conway, watched through his black binoculars as Peter and two armed guards made their way into a local Starbucks. From his surveillance he had learned that Peter had to have coffee and he preferred it to come from Starbucks, and he was a nightly visitor of a local gym.

However, this night Peter wanted to jog through the beautiful Rock Creek Park. After a few moments of recording and scoping out the park's layout, Mike disappeared in the calmness and darkness of the night.

Chapter 11
Managua, Nicaragua...

Jose and Rico Gomez walked about without a care in the world. After the two brothers testified against Face, they murdered the F.B.I. agents who were protecting them in the safe house; and then escaped back to their home land of Nicaragua. Neither of the brothers expected Face to get off, they had him written off before the trial even materialized. From what they knew about the U.S. and those who went against the Federal Government, nobody beat the system; but with Face they had gotten it all wrong.

Now they were wanted by the U.S. Federal Marshalls. The two knew they could never step a foot back on U.S. soil. Their faces were plastered all over posters showing they were two members of the F.B.I.'s most wanted list; but as long as they stayed on their turf they had no worries. The Nicaraguan government was on their payroll and they were never going to be extradited. They were free and clear and living as kings.

The three plus years that they were on the run did not damper their positions in the drug ring. Their names were tainted but they still were two of the biggest dealers in the game. Sitting on the porch of their beach home villa, the brothers began discussing their new Columbian connect.

"With the Columbians as our partners we will be ten times bigger and even more powerful than we were before" Jose said, as he sipped on his glass of red wine and he reclined in his comfortable patio chair. "You're right but there is something about Roberto that worries me. He seems too eager to work with us" Rico said, laying deeper into the portable hammock. "Stop worrying brother, everything will be fine. He's a criminal just like us, plus the U.S. wants him too" Jose said, laughing away any concern his brother was showing. "I know that there is something about him that I just don't like. Maybe it's that cheap shirt he had on the other day but I just don't like the guy." Jose walked over to his brother and said, "His fucking shirt brother, who cares how he dresses. He will make us money and the more we make the better he'll look." Rico started to loosen up his apprehension as Jose continued. "We've made plenty of money with the Columbians and we're untouchable. We've got security, informants, and the world is ours", Jose shouted. A small grin appeared upon Rico's face as he picked up the bowel of mangles off the small wicker table. "Yes, brother you are right...the world is ours."

**Temple University
Philadelphia, PA...**

Inside of the Charles Klein Law building, Arianna sat in the library typing on her laptop computer. At least once a day she would Google the name Norman "Face" Smith Jr. to see what new information would surface. She studied him as if he was a class assignment. She wanted to know everything about the man who had killed her parents;

who happened to be the same man who was her brother's older brother.

As she continued to search she thought about what he did daily, how his children and his wife were, what they looked like, what he thought about, if he cared about the murders he committed; and with the memory of her parents lying dead she collapsed her face onto the desk and began to sob quietly.

She reached for a tissue to clean her face, once she heard the footsteps of a classmate approaching. She gathered herself but the memories of the day were vivid. She could remember hearing the words "What about the children" as well as seeing the lifeless bodies of her parents slumped over.

It was like it all happened yesterday. Her parents were tortured and she could hear her mother's voice, begging to be let go. She could feel the white pillowcase that had been placed over her head and she was suffocating. These memories enraged her and like her older brother Robbie, she was determined to see Face and make him pay for all he had taken from them. She didn't know what she would do but she knew he had to suffer.

Arianna did what she could to release her rage and deal with her emotions. Robbie and she would talk often and she knew about Face's mom and how she had treated Robbie, and sometimes just thinking about Pamela would set her off. Twice a week she met with a therapist but she didn't understand why the rage was still elevated. She cried her eyes out to this woman, yelled, screamed and still she was angry and wanted Face dead.

A few weeks earlier she had purchased a 9mm with the intent of killing herself. The pain had mounted on her shoulders and no one understood what she was dealing with. She knew that her brother had experienced the loss as well but she saw that he was better at handling his emotions. She felt defenseless, weak, and completely hopeless; but a phone call from her brother telling her he loved her saved her from ending her life. She took it as a sign not to pull the trigger because it was a random call that came in as she was holding the gun to her head.

Arianna logged off of her laptop and pulled the screen down, as she packed up and got ready to go to her hour long therapist session.

Chapter 12
Broad & Fairmount...

Face, Reese, and Quincy all sat around the living room of one of Face's hideaways. The three were the only ones who knew about this place. Face was bringing Reese up to date with everything that has transpired. He listened intensely and without interruption as Face emphasized the importance of him staying focused and on track. "It's us against them and they won't stop until one of us fucks up and gives them a way to take us down. We were lucky last time but I'm not about to let luck decide where I go in life. From here on out we do shit right and without fault. I'm too high up to be dragged down for some sucka-shit."

Reese understood and he was overwhelmed by all the information he had just absorbed. He was still taken back by Peter J. Greenberg. He just couldn't believe that Peter got Face for 500 million dollars. He was a little upset that Face didn't tell him this before now, but Face explained to him that he didn't want to tell him too much while he was locked up. He knew just being incarcerated was a burden in itself.

"So we got a lot of enemies. The list looks hella long and at the top is Peter" Reese said, looking at Face and then continuing. "And we got the Gomez brothers, Watson, Truck, Agent Powaski and McDonald and that Ron Perry nigga. I have to do him myself! He killed Momma and DJ and there ain't a nigga alive that's gonna tell me he gets to walk the streets on chill."

Reese was becoming irate. Ron Perry was a great source of anger for him and he wanted him bumped to the top of the list. Quincy tried to console him when he said, "We're going to get them all. We already had Doc take care of Agent Powaski and McDonald's wife. We'll get those agents shortly too." Reese nodded his head because he was too frustrated to talk about their living enemies anymore. Too many people had tried them and he wanted to protect his team. There was no way this was going to continue on his watch.

"So what's the good news" Reese asked, looking at Quincy. Face took over the conversation and said, "Well, we have a new connect. His name is Roberto Fuentes and he's from Columbia. He's in the Los Rostrojas Cartel and they're the largest supplier out." Reese smiled; he was always pleased to hear about the family making money and powerful connections.

"Damn, that's what I'm talking about fellas" Reese said, giving both of his friends a hug. "So you ready" Face asked. Reese looked at Quincy because he wasn't sure what Face was talking about. "Ready for what..." he asked. "For our trip out to the Bahamas. We leave in the morning, we got a connect to meet up with." Reese stood confident when he said, "No doubt."

Suite 514
The Hilton Hotel
Washington, D.C...

Inside of a private suite on the 5th floor of the Hilton Hotel, Peter J. Greenberg sat in front of his laptop computer as he distributed 500 million dollars into the account of C.W. Watson and another 500 million to Paul Warner. He was supposed to make the billion dollar transfer earlier but due to bank securities and verifications, it took a while to get his clearances.

"Are we wealthy men yet" Paul asked, as he stood up and walked over to Peter. Peter was disgusted with Paul and Watson even though he still had a few billion in his accounts. He quickly closed his transaction and said "Yes, the money is in there now".

Paul took the computer and quickly logged onto his foreign bank account and checked his balance. His face was beaming as he saw how quickly he had become wealthier than he had ever been in his life. This was the part of his job he loved. Previously he had only scored several thousand dollars here and there, but now, thanks to his dedication and Watson's trust in him, he had officially crossed over and was never looking to come back. Paul stood up and walked out of the room with a smile on his face that could light up a neighborhood during a blackout.

Peter walked over to the bed and lay down. He knew something wasn't right with Paul and Watson, he knew they were just as crooked as him; if not worse. Peter wanted to get this entire situation behind him and never look back again. He had enough money to go to a country that wouldn't extradite him and he was willing to leave any and everything behind to make him a new life. For the moment he felt safe because the government was protecting him but he knew he had to get away soon because Face was a highly connected man.

Inside a tinted black limousine, Paul Warner set beside C.W. Watson with a big grin plastered on his face.

"It's done" Paul said.

"He really thinks we brought him back here to get Face" Paul added.

"Good but remember this information is strictly between us. If this gets out my political career goes down the toilet."

"My lips are sealed and we don't have to worry about Peter. He's a thief with a bounty on his head. Once he leaves he's never going to come back to the States."

"Good. We'll just keep him around for a few more weeks to convince him Face is the reason he's here."

"No problem, but if you decide we should wipe him out and take all he's got just say the word. I'm ready."

"I think we'll let the coward stick around, we don't want to get our hands too dirty."

The two men shook hands and as soon as Paul exited the limo, it pulled off going in the opposite direction in which he was walking.

Chapter 13
Chestnut Hill, PA…

As Pamela sat in the living room of her elegant Chestnut Hill home, she heard a strange noise coming from her backyard. She immediately reached under her sofa and pulled out a loaded .380 pistol and headed towards the kitchen. Though her home had a security system installed she knew she had to be cautious.

With her gun clutched in her hand, she nervously peeped through the curtains to find the source of the noise. In the darkness of the night she could see a shadowy image running away. Pamela couldn't tell if she had just seen a raccoon or if someone was snooping around her home. After checking all of her doors and windows, she went to her alarm panel and ensured it was properly armed.

She walked upstairs to her bedroom but was unable to fall asleep. She laid there with her gun in her hand ready to defend herself is she had to. Through her fear her mind wandered back to a time when she had a man in her life. It had been quite some time since she had the companionship that she currently desired. She thought of Norman, Mouse and Jay often.

Since Jay's suicide she had felt broken. She was uncertain if she'd every find a man who could love her, respect and accept who she truly was. For now all she had was her pictures and memories. She knew if someone did come along, she wouldn't be so afraid at night and wouldn't have to sleep with her man of steel; which was her loaded .380.

Southwest Philly...

The green and white sign read "Welcome to Philadelphia" and Truck felt his body explode with fear as he crossed into the city limits. It had been over ten years since Truck had been in his old stomping grounds. The time he served in prison and his time in the witness protection program had kept him away.

Although he was back and had missed his hood, he knew he had to keep a low profile. He had gotten word that there was a million dollar bounty on his head, and if the wrong person saw him he would be shot on the spot. Then there were those who might take him out simply because he had defied the code of the streets. The streets had copies of the transcripts from the courts, and most people had read everything Truck said against Face and Reese.

As Truck drove down Woodland Avenue, he saw that his city had changed. It appeared that things had gotten worse than before and so many buildings were dilapidated, and black-owned businesses he used to frequent had shut down. Truck noticed that the drug-dealers had gotten younger and even they seemed to be in a Zombie state; just like the addicts they served.

Truck drove up to Greenway Avenue and got caught at a red light. Seeing a heroin addict, he looked at him as he ran around in a circle and was skitzing out of his mind. "Damn, what have I gotten myself into" he said, before pulling off when the light turned green.

Chapter 14
Center City Philadelphia...

Veronica had Carter straddled beneath her, as she rode his thick, long dick like a seasoned cowgirl. Together their moans filled the air of her bedroom and the sweet scent of sex covered the two. Carter was such a good fuck and Veronica enjoyed the sex more than the money she was getting. He was one of her clients who were actually worth the bang and it was a nice change; compared to the older clientele who had little dicks and shorter stamina.

As their naked bodies were covered in sweat, the two gave in and shared another powerful orgasm. Veronica slumped down beside Carter, breathing hard and heavy. "Wow" she exclaimed. "I truly needed that" she smiled. "Me too" Carter said, as he wiped the sweat from his forehead.

Later on that night as Veronica slept peacefully in her bed; Carter quietly picked up his cellphone and crept out to the bathroom. After closing the bathroom door he sent someone a text message. Within a minute he had gotten a response and after reading it he shut his Blackberry phone off.

Carter did his best to tip-toe back into the room as he climbed into the bed. Veronica rolled over and placed her hands on his chest before whispering "I can smell a married man. Just make sure she doesn't get my number or find out my address." She rolled over and began to fall back asleep. Carter didn't respond, instead he curled up behind her and readied his body for sleep.

Silver Springs, Maryland...

For over a year Mike Conway had covertly watched every single move C.W. Watson made. There was nothing about the Senator that he didn't know. Recently, Senator Watson had been spending a lot of time with a mysterious short, stocky man and occasionally he visited the Vice President. Mike had taken pictures of the two and stored them on his flash-drive. Currently he didn't have any information on the man but he knew he would soon have all he needed to identify the mystery man.

As he looked through the lenses of his binoculars, Mike watched as Watson walked throughout his home. Even though he was a distance away, his equipment was advanced and it was like he was standing as close as the porch.

Watson was a man of routine, so after dinner he'd watch TV in the living room, and then it was upstairs to bed with his wife. They rarely made love and if they did it was once in a blue. Like many other politicians in D.C., Watson had a beautiful young mistress who satisfied most of his sexual urges. The two would meet in the Hilton, the same hotel that Peter J. Greenberg was staying in; and he had his way with the vivacious young lady.

Mike had all the information he needed on C.W. Watson to come to his own conclusion. In his opinion Watson was just another corrupt politician that would soon choke off of his own lies and crumble.

Kamalame Cay, Bahamas...

In the Island of Paradise, Roberto Fuentes owned a charming, Roman inspired villa on the waterfront. He was quite the propertier; he owned numerous properties on three different continents and in twelve countries throughout the world.

As the small army of armed men surrounded his home, Roberto, Face and Reese sat in the living room eating and having drinks.

"It's such a pleasure to meet you Reese."

"Same here."

"Face has told me a great deal about you and I respect your loyalty."

"Thank you, I take being loyal real personal. It's what I live by."

"Is there any other way" Roberto, said smiling and sipping on his cognac.

"Fellas, I want to get down to business. Your former connect, the Gomez brothers, were giving you two thousand kilos each buy…correct" Roberto asked, waiting for their reply.

"Yes, about that…" Face began, but was interrupted by Roberto.

"Well, those days are behind us. In a week I will let you know where to pick up a shipment of 5,000 kilos of the purest cocaine around, and 1,000 kilos of heroin will also be a part of that shipment. The location will be in Philadelphia and you should make all arrangements to be sure no one is tailing you, and if anything feels off let me know."

Face and Reese eyes had lit up. This was surely a better situation than before and the largest shipment that they had ever received.

"Face I understand that you have a loyal crew in
Miami, New York, LA, Chicago, Detroit and your
hometown…so you should be able to take back
what was yours."

Face grinned and asked, "So what's the price".

"Gentlemen follow me outside", Roberto said, as
everyone came on the porch.

"Face, remember when I told you I respect you. That
you are a stand-up man."

"Yeah, you tell me that all the time" Face said,
smiling.

"Well that loyalty means a lot to me, and I think you
should be compensated."

"Roberto, what does that mean man" Face, asked.

"It means that two hundred kilos of heroin is a gift
from me and you can keep the twenty five hundred
kilos of the cocaine too. The other half I expect
payment of seven thousand per kilo. I know you
guys are good at math so I won't insult you by
giving you the final figure."

Face and Reese were shocked. It was a good
deal, no it was a great deal and there was no way he
could be serious.

"Is this some type of joke" Face asked.

"No, I don't play jokes. This is a deal and a sign of
my respect. Not too many take on the U.S.
Government and win. I watched the entire case and
have it on DVD too. Nowadays every man that gets
questioned tells on everyone, but not you. You
could have taken everyone down but that's not who
you are. This is a token of my appreciation."

"Thank you Roberto" Face said.

"No, thank you. You two are soldiers and understand

that snitches have no place in our business."

As the conversation over the new shipment came to a close, a Rolls Royce pulled up and they all got inside. As the car drove down the road, Face asked Roberto "Did you hear anything on the Gomez brothers". Roberto smiled and said, "I'm glad you asked, you'll be meeting them tomorrow afternoon". Reese couldn't believe it and neither could Face. "Are you serious…" Reese asked. Roberto looked to him and lightheartedly said, "Of course, remember I don't play jokes. They will be here and the best thing about that is they don't know you two are here. I don't play jokes but I do love a good surprise."

Face and Reese just looked at each other as they thought about the upcoming day. Scores would be settled and they didn't know what they would do but they knew the brothers had to be dealt with.

"Tomorrow you fellas can deal with them any way you like. I used to have a great deal of respect for them but once I saw they had loose tongues and no honor, they are dead to me. But for now let's eat and enjoy Paradise."

Agents McDonald and Powaski had been all over the city searching for clues that would put a face on the killer. They had put the heat on every drug strip and had questioned every felon they could get their hands on. Desperation was all over them and they had left their business cards in barbershops, hair salons, Laundromats and local bars.

As they made their way back to their offices on 6th Street, Agent Powaski phone rang.

"Agent Powaski."

"Hi, my name is Raheem Davis and I need to speak to Agent Powaski."

"Yes, this is him, how can I help you?"

"I'm calling about…about the two women that were murdered recently. I found your card in a barbershop on 42nd and Lancaster."

"What information do you have!" he demanded.

"Well, I rather not say on the phone but can we meet up today?"

"Listen, you need to understand this case is very serious.

Do you have information or not?"

"Yes, I heard someone talking about the two dead women and I think this information can help your case."

"Okay, where are you?"

"I'm in West Philly, my address is 944 N 43rd Street."

"Okay, I'm on my way."

"What's your number, the caller id blocked?"

"I don't have a phone, I'm using a payphone."

"No problem, I'll see you in a about an hour."

McDonald could tell when his partner was weary of the information that was called in. Lately crack heads had been trying to scrounge up a few dollars by providing useless information and they were getting tired of checking out those dead-end sources.

"What do you want to do", McDonald asked. His Partner was noticeably frustrated by the call.

"Well we have to go up West Philly. I'm just sick of these scumbags trying to get us to support their habit. They never have a phone and they always want to meet in person because they want money. And for what! They don't give up shit." Agent McDonald understood and felt the same way but he knew if they wanted to solve this case they had to check out any possible leads; even if they were inadequate.

McDonald made a quick U-turn and they made their way up to West Philly.

Paul Warner sat in front of his computer staring at the screen. He still couldn't believe that he had 500 million dollars in his account. It was the most money he had ever had in his life and he was mesmerized by the amount sitting in his account. He wanted more and greed had converted his soul.

Paul Warner was nothing more than a crook and a murderer. He had killed over thirty men, women and some children and was always eager to add more people to his body count. He was a sick man who had the protection of the government on his side.

Chapter 15
Downtown Philly...

Pamela pulled her BMW into the parking lot of the T & F Real Estate Firm. She had an afternoon meeting with Tasha and Veronica; so they decided to meet up at Tasha's office for lunch and some good ole chatting. The ladies enjoyed being amongst each other and felt too often they were the only ones they could trust. They had no intention of opening up their circle so they kept it tight and made sure they stayed active and in touch with one another.

When Pamela got out of her car she had noticed a strange looking young man standing just a short distance away from where she had parked; and he was staring intently at her. She stood frozen for a minute as she wondered what the hell he was looking at, but soon she realized she was looking at someone who was quite familiar. He was a tall, dark, muscular man and his face was identical to one she had seen before.

She began to tremble and was filled with fear. "Hello mother" Robbie said. Pamela couldn't respond. Her mind was racing with thoughts of confusion. She was nervous. Why had he decided to show up now, what did he want? Pamela saw Hood all in his face and the thought of the rape came rushing back into her mind. "Hello mother, do you remember me" he asked.

As he removed his hands from his pocket, she could see that he had a gun in his hands. He pointed the gun at her stomach and before she could utter a word, he had squeezed the trigger on the Glock 9mm three times. The bullets entered into Pam's flesh and as she screamed, her body slumped to the ground.

Robbie made his escape by running through the parking lot and Pamela's screams echoed into the air. While Pamela lay on the ground shocked and in pain, Veronica had just pulled into the lot. She saw a tall man running away in the distance and thought she noticed his face, but turned her attention to parking her vehicle. As she turned down her music, which had been turned up to the highest volume, she heard the voice of her best friend screaming for help.

Immediately she threw the gear into park and jumped out to see where the screams were coming from. As she searched the parking lot she couldn't believe her eyes when she came across Pamela, who was bloody and curled up in pain. Tears fell from her eyes instantly as she rushed to comfort her friend and Veronica screamed out for help.

Veronica could barely get herself together. She kneeled down and tried to pick up her friend but Pamela screamed because she was in severe pain. Veronica didn't want this to be true and as she struggled to call for help, two onlookers who were walking by came running to help out. One immediately called the police and the other tried to keep Pamela conscious by asking her name and how she was.

Pamela looked up at Veronica and said "It was Robbie...it was my son Robbie" before closing her eyes and slumping into Veronica's arms.

Robbie ran through a series of alleys and headed towards the heart of Chinatown. As he walked down 9th and Race Street he spotted the dark blue Chevy Impala parked at the corner. He rushed to the car and jumped inside and said "Drive...drive, hurry up and get me out of here!!!" Ron Perry asked no questions as he sped on the gas and maneuvered his way quickly through the streets.

When they pulled onto Broad and Spring Garden Street, Ron Perry asked "Did you get her?" Robbie, who was still a bit shaken up had hesitated to respond but soon said "Yeah, I shot her three times. I caught her as soon as she was getting out of the car." Ron Perry placed his hand on Robbie's shoulder and said "Good job Robbie, your father would've been so proud of you."

Robbie had started to realize what he had just done. He had been holding so much anger inside of him and now that some of it had been released he said, "Yeah fuck that bitch...she deserves nothing but death." Ron Perry nodded his head in agreement and said "Now her son is next."

Robbie sat back in the passenger seat and felt somewhat satisfied with his actions. He had no love for the woman who had treated him horrible. She never wanted him and had made the mistake of not getting an abortion with him. Today he had felt vindicated and all the planning, sneaking around her home, and following her had paid off.

When Ron Perry pulled to the corner of 17th and Spring Garden Street, Robbie got out of his car and climbed into his Mercedes Benz. Arianna was seated inside waiting for him.

"I got her" he said, as he started up the car then turned down the new Inner City Hustlers cd that was playing. "I shot her three times" he said, looking at Arianna as she began to show her pleasure by sporting a light grin.

As she leaned over to give her brother a hug, she was glad that he had released some of his anger. She had grown-up with Robbie and felt all the pain he held inside. Robbie had always felt unwanted and longed for a mother who would show him true love and affection; and one he could have a bond with. He once had felt that but that woman was taken from him when his step-mother was murdered.

Robbie lifted his head up from off of his sister's shoulder and said "I feel really good now. I feel like I got that bitch good and now Face will feel what we felt all these years." Arianna looked into her brother's eyes and she could see a burden had been lifted off of his shoulders...but she knew that this was only the beginning. Face would have to be dealt with or they would be the ones looking death in the eyes.

As he slowly drove away Robbie turned the music back up and let the sounds of the Inner City Hustlers soothe his nervousness.

Chapter 16
West Philadelphia...

Agent McDonald pulled up in front of the old row home on 43rd Street and parked the car. Agent Powaski and he got out of the car and walked up on to the porch. Cautious and unaware of who was the informant, they looked around to scope the scenery before knocking on the door.

No one answered and as they looked around the dilapidated neighborhood the only one outside was an old disheveled woman. Powaski knocked harder and within a few moments a young raggedy looking man answered the door and said, "Come on in."

They followed the man inside and from the looks of the place they knew they would be standing up the entire time. As they entered the dining room, the man sat at the table and offered them a seat; however they refused and McDonald began his search for answers.

"So Raheem, tell us what you know."

"Well a few days ago I was at the barbershop on Lancaster Ave and I heard this man and this lady talking about two women who had got killed."

Powaski took notes as a knock came at the door. Raheem excused himself from the table and went to to see who was knocking.

"Grandma, I'll come over in a minute I'm busy now."

"What" she yelled.

"Grandma I'm busy right now."

"What you in trouble again boy."

"No mam. It's nothing like that. I'll talk to you later."
 He said loudly.

"Grandma, I said it's cool."

"Okay" she said.

As he made his way back into the dining room, the agents looked to ensure no one else was behind him.

"Okay Raheem, let's get down to business. What did you hear?"

He sat back down at the table and said "Two people were talking about the murders. They said they knew who did it." The agents' eyes widened as they begin to take this tip serious.

Seconds later the old woman appeared, surprising the agents but what was more startling was that she was holding and aiming a 9mm at both agents. Raheem reached under the table and grabbed his handgun that was hidden in a compartment under the table, and pointed it at the agents at well.

"What's going on here" Agent Powaski asked. Grandma removed her wig and the two men realized they had been set-up. All the tips that had poured in to the agents were phony and Quincy had been behind the entire scam. He yelled for the agents to put their hands up, as two armed men came out the closet.

Now there were four men armed and ready to fire on the agents. Raheem searched them and removed their guns. They were enraged and filled with disbelief. Why hadn't they been more in tune with this scheme?

"What's this all about" Agent Powaski demanded.

"Face, you remember him right" Qunicy said.

   Their eyes both lit up.

"Norman "Face" Smith Jr." McDonald asked.

"Yes, that's him" Quincy said.

"We haven't heard from him in years. What's the beef?" Powaski asked.

"This isn't about meat, no, it's all about revenge" Quincy responded.

   Quincy stepped away from the agents and the two armed men who had come out of the closets begin firing. The guns both had silencer attached so no one could hear the firing squad empting their clips. Even the screams of the agents were quickly silenced as the bullets bounced through and out of their bodies.

   Once the men were lying on the floor dead, Quincy instructed the three men to clean up the mess and get rid of the car. Raheem whose real name was Kyle was already on it. He quickly pulled out a saw and began to cut the bodies up-so they could fit into the forty-gallon, black construction bags. He was a killer in his own right and expert at getting rid of bodies.

   Quincy headed towards the backdoor and got inside of his tinted Dodge Magnum wagon. He drove down Girard Avenue so he could make his way back to North Philly.

Hahnemann University Hospital...

   Veronica and Tasha nervously paced back and forth inside the crowded emergency room. Doctors were desperately working to save Pamela's life. When the paramedics had arrived, her pulse was so weak they couldn't detect it and were performing CPR the entire ride to the hospital. Pamela had been shot at close range, three times in her abdominal area. No one was sure if she would make it and Tasha had been trying frantically to reach Face.

Face was out of town with Reese taking care of business in the Bahamas. She knew while he was away on business he didn't want to be bothered and under normal circumstances she would respect his wishes, but now she needed to contact him. His mother was clinging to life and had been shot by her own son.

Veronica was numb and unable to say much. She just paced and when she tried to pray she couldn't think of what to say. Her mind was racing and she had blanked out. She sat on the floor and began to hyperventilate. As Tasha turned around to ask if she was alright, she saw Veronica on the ground and she looked like she was about to have a seizure. Tasha screamed for the nurse and when the nurse arrived she saw Veronica foaming at the mouth. She rushed to the nurse's station to get assistance from a doctor.

Chapter 17

We have breaking news this afternoon. In downtown Philadelphia at the respected Real Estate office of T&F, the mother of rumored drug Kingpin Norman "Face" Smith Jr. has been shot numerous times and rushed to Hahnemann University hospital. The incident occurred earlier this afternoon in the real estate's parking lot and no suspects have been named or apprehended. She is listed in critical condition and we will keep you updated as soon as we have more on this story.

Truck had been listening to KYW1060 News radio while driving around in his truck. He was stunned to hear the news and didn't know who would have shot Pamela. He knew how close Face was to his mother and knew who ever had shot Pam, would have been better off committing suicide.

Truck continued driving towards South Philly. He was about to meet up with his cousin who had a loaded gun and some money for him. As he continued to drive he wanted to know who had it out for Pamela. He knew Face was about to spit fire if he wasn't on it already.

Later That Night...

Kyle and the two other men had removed the clothes from the bodies and bagged up the dissected body parts of Agent Powaski and Agent McDonald. With the cover of darkness upon them, they placed the bags containing the bodies in the back of the Agents' car.

Kyle and one of the armed men made their way to a small street right off of Wissahickon and Chelten; while the other man followed in a car behind them. It was a backstreet with no houses and it was a dead-end due to a sink hole that had ruined the abandoned street many years ago.

As the trio exited the vehicles, the agents' car was drenched with acid and doused with gasoline. The bags were opened and the bodies were also soaked with gasoline and acid; a mixture that immediately started to eat the flesh and right through the bags.

Once the car and the bodies were covered with the chemicals, Kyle lit the bag containing the agents' clothes and threw it in the car. They stood back as the car became engulfed in flames and as they walked towards their car, the agents' car exploded. They all turned around amazed at how quickly the car had blown up, and the flames coming from the car were so hot they could feel the fire on their faces.

Once in the car Kyle phoned Quincy.

"Hey man, it's all taken care of."

"Good, so there's no evidence right."

"No, nothing."

"Cool, I'll talk to you later."

Feeling rushed off the phone Kyle sensed something was wrong.

"Yo, what's up Q?"

"Shit is crazy. The boss mom got shot up bad. I can't get in touch with him."

"What!"

"Yeah, shit is fucked up right now. Yo, but I'll call
you once…I'll call you back. "
The phone line was silent.

Washington, D.C…

Peter J. Greenberg did his best to push the
scandal out of his mind as he began his late-night jog.
His mind had been clouded with racing thoughts of
deceit and the trickery C.W. Watson and Paul Warner
had implemented upon him. These scoundrels had
used the intelligence and power of the U.S.
Government to bring him back to the states and stole
a billion dollars from him without anyone noticing;
and there was no one to stop them.
As the two armed bodyguards escorted him to
the park, he wished he knew a way to make Watson
and Warner pay. He wanted to find a way to have
them imprisoned and brought to justice, but how
could he do that without implicating himself he
wondered. For now he laced up his sneakers and
began to jog, hoping it would bring some calmness to
his mind and relief to his tense body.
Unbeknownst to Peter his every move was
being monitored and the night-vision goggles could
see clearly through the dimly light pathways he ran
upon. Mike Conway was deep into his mission and
had given Face all the details on where Peter ate, who
he talked to, what he wore, and how nightly jogging
had become a norm for him.
Mike didn't know everything about Peter
though because Face didn't give him all details. Mike
had wondered what the government wanted with

Peter because he stayed connected to his former Intel buddies and nothing was on the radar with him. He knew something big was going on though because the twenty-four hours of protected service wouldn't be given to just any average Joe; and these guards were very professional and skilled so he knew they had to be from the U.S. Marshalls, The C.I.A. or the F.B.I.

After more surveillance on Peter, Mike wrote down some notes and left a coded message for Face. He knew Face and Reese were out of town and their cellphones were turned off for international security reasons.

In the darkness of the night, Mike placed his goggles under his leather jacket and calmly walked back towards his new home; which was the luxurious Hilton Hotel. He was now staying in Suite 515, in a room next to Peter J. Greenberg.

Chapter 18
Early the Next Morning
6th and Arch Streets...

The pressure at the F.B.I. office had escalated to its highest level. The entire building was in a complete panic because four people connected with the bureau had been murdered. They had lost two agents and those agent's wives as well. With no evidence or tips to lead them to the killer or killers, headquarters in Washington, D.C. sent a team of twenty special agents to assist in cracking this case. The Philadelphia Police Department has also offered to assist with any field work they could, and by putting officers out on the streets they were hopeful they would come upon some information.

This was the biggest story on the East Coast and not only was it covered on the local news stations but CNN and MSNBC had also picked up the story. The F.B.I. was on their highest alert since the World Trade Center terrorist attacks.

With all the commotion going on in the building, Karen Brown sat calmly at her desk typing. She worked as if she had no worries in the world and all she thought about was meeting up with Quincy later on that night. Nothing else much matter to the love struck woman.

Inside the comforts of his moderate sized row-home, Doc sat back on the sofa watching the local early morning news. Every morning after a shower and a strong cup of black coffee, this was his normal routine. When Doc wasn't torturing, murdering, or eating the eyeballs of his dead victims, he enjoyed watching the news or CSI.

Doc loved information and although he had plenty of books to read, he had gotten away from a once avid hobby. Doc's IQ was measured to be over 120 and he surely showed signs of high intelligence, but many in his neighborhood labeled him as an old, weird, white guy who was creepy but cool.

Doc had a love for poor people and many in his neighborhood where blacks who had no health insurance. Instead of going to their local hospitals or clinics, they'd always go to Doc first to see if he could fix them up for free; and Doc loved the appreciation his patients showed him. He loved that once they got to know him they no longer judged him, and they didn't hesitate to call him if they needed his medical care.

As the news flashed the story on Pamela's shooting Doc couldn't believe his eyes. Who had done this to his friend's mother? He started to cry and was visible angry. He cut the TV off and said aloud "Don't worry Face; Doc will take care of whoever did his. Trust me my good friend, Doc will get them."

Hahnemann University Hospital...

Ron Perry walked through the emergency sliding doors and stood by one of the large vending machines that lined the wall. As he waited and watched, he noticed the halls were filled with RN's, doctors, and other hospital staff members. A few moments later a short black man dressed as an orderly walked over to Ron Perry and the two shook hands.

"Hey, let's walk over to the cafeteria" the man suggested. Both men walked down the hallway and entered the crowded cafeteria. They found a small table in the back and sat down.

"Hungry?"

"No, I'm fine. I had a cheesesteak from Geno's" Ron Perry said.

"So, what's the situation?" Ron whispered.

"It's not looking good for her. She's still critical and in a medical induced coma."

"Has Face shown up?"

"No, I haven't seen him since his mom was admitted."

Ron sat up because he was confused. Why wouldn't Face show up to see what was going on with his own mother? Something certainly didn't sound right.

"Are you sure?"

"I'm positive, he hasn't been here. Maybe it's too much for him to handle."

"No, this isn't like him. She's his life" Ron Perry said.

"Listen, I'm not sure why he hasn't visited but I'll call you if he shows up or if something changes with his mom."

"Alright, has anyone else come to see her."

"No, just the two ladies who came in with her. The older woman almost seized out. The doctors had to admit her for a day but she's okay now. Oh and the only other person was the dude with the stern face."

"Did you manage to find out his name?"

"No, he's only here for a few minutes and then he rushes out."

"Okay, just stay up on this and let me know asap of any updates."

"I will Ron."

When the conversation ended both men stood up from the table and exited the cafeteria in different directions. Ron Perry walked out the hospital to his car and the man walked to a waiting elevator and got on. He worked at the hospital but also for Ron Perry as a secret informant.

Once the elevator reached the 3rd floor he exited the elevator and calmly walked past Pamela's room. He glanced inside and immediately noticed Tasha and Veronica by Pamela's side. They were crying and praying, and Tasha had brought a bible to read a few scriptures to Pamela.

Chapter 19
Kamalame Cay, Bahamas...

Rico and Jose Gomez stood outside the Yacht and watched as it pulled up to the private pier. When they stepped off the boat a black limousine was awaiting them. The driver immediately introduced himself as Sergio and opened the backdoor for the brothers. As the two brothers entered the limo they relaxed in the backseat and had a glass of champagne; and the car drove off down the dusty road.

The Gomez brothers were excited to be in the Bahamas. Though they loved the beautiful island, they were more thrilled about the business deal they were about to negotiate. For the brothers to secure the shipment of one hundred thousand kilos of Columbia's number one import was surely something that would make them a lot more money; and bring them the power which they craved.

The limo headed to the home of Roberto Fuentes and the brothers comfortably sat in the car discussing the impending deal and their perkier futures. They were like two kids in a candy store with a hundred dollars in their pockets, and no parental supervision.

Within just a few minutes the car had pulled up to the home of Roberto Fuentes. Sergio exited the limo and went to the back door to open it for the brothers. As they exited the limo, they saw Roberto standing on the front porch dressed in a colorful beach shirt and a long pair of white shorts.

"Welcome to my home" Roberto said, receiving the brothers and ushering them to come in. As the brothers walked upon the porch they all shook hands, and Jose said "Thanks for inviting us to your home. It's simply beautiful." Roberto was flattered and the brothers took notice of the armed guards who secured the home and the perimeter. Roberto led the men around to the backyard where a nice spread of food and wine, and scotch had been set up.

Once everyone was seated and enjoying the light feast, Roberto said "So fellas, in our last conversation I believe we were comfortable with one hundred thousand kilos to get us started". Both brothers were delighted and smiled. "Yes, that will be perfect. You know we are still getting ourselves together and getting back on track. After that mess in the states we have had a few bumps, but this will surely put us back were we belong" Rico said.

Roberto nodded his head and said" That's something I'd like to talk to you guys about. I mean I'm very curious to know what actually happened…why were you two helping the U.S. Government?" Both brothers didn't like the tone of his voice and had heard that tone from their other associates who were upset with them over their choice to cooperate with the government.

Jose became quite serious and said "It was very simple. We were looking at a lifetime sentence for a nigga that wasn't our blood. He had his shit fucked up and got us involved. We didn't like what we did but we did what we had to." Roberto didn't say anything he just looked on as Rico said "Why are we talking about Face anyway? He won his case and

96

we wish him the best. He's a good man and he made us some money and we made him money too, so in my eyes we are even. Today is a new day, you know."

Roberto stood up and said "Yes, today is a new day but old memories never die." He smiled as the brothers had a puzzled look glued to their faces. They didn't know what he was talking about and felt uncomfortable. "What is going on" Jose asked, as he stood up. Roberto looked deep into his eyes and said "Loyalty is what is going on! Real men live by it and rats will die without it… Come out my friends!"

The brothers were both standing and fear had comprised their bodies. Face and Reese walked up on the men from a hidden side entrance. The brothers didn't know what to do but before they could reach for any weapons, the armed guards had approached them with guns pressed to their backs.

"Face please" Rico said, but was told to shut up by Reese. Rico fell to his knees and began to beg for his life and Jose followed suit. Roberto and his men backed off and left without uttering a word. This was a situation that had to be handled by Face and Reese.

Rico cried out for mercy and begged for forgiveness. He offered money and land but nothing was going to change the outcome of this meeting. Reese shouted "Die like fucking men you rats" before spitting on them. He pointed the gun at Jose's head and then at Rico's head.

Face just watched the brothers groveling at his feet. He had made them more money than they could count and in return they had turned on him. He replayed the memory of the two brothers sitting on the witness stand testifying against him and the taste in his mouth was so sour. What did he need to say to these men he thought, but he knew all that needed to be said was being spoken from the sizzle in his eyes?

"Which one of your muthafuckas wants to go first" Reese asked, delighting in the fear the brothers were displaying. Reese called to Face and told him to hand him his gun. He said "They told together, they should die at the same damn time", and then he pulled the triggers on both hand guns; sending slugs directly into the skulls of Jose and Rico Gomez.

Reese continued shooting, emptying the clips and sending the bullets into their heads and bodies; until they lay lifeless in the backyard of Roberto Fuentes home. Reese wasn't satisfied with just shooting them, so he pistol whipped the men until their heads caved in. He had gotten so caught up in the beatings that he slipped on the pool of blood that had surrounded their bodies. As he lay on his back laughing, the reign of the Gomez brothers was no more.

Face and Reese walked into the house and Roberto had his maid show Reese to the bathroom so he could wash and get out of his bloody clothes. "Get rid of these scumbags" Roberto instructed his men, as he reached to Face and said "My loyal friend, we will get you back to the position where you belong." Face extended his hand and as they shook, Roberto said, "Welcome to my family and you'll never have to question my loyalty. I'd rather die than cross my family." Face nodded and said "Me too."

Twenty minutes later Reese came downstairs and joined the men on the porch. "That shower felt good, now can we get something to eat I'm fucking starving" he said, as the men started laughing. Roberto smiled and said, "Sure, just let me check on the work being done in the yard."

As they followed him in the yard they saw that his men had used machetes to chop of the heads of the Gomez brothers. Out of curiosity Reese asked, "What are you going to do with the heads" and Roberto replied, "The sharks have to eat, so why not feed the sharks to the sharks."

Reese laughed and was upbeat. However; Face had an unnerving feeling that had plagued him all day. He couldn't fully enjoy being rid of the Gomez brothers. Face kept quiet most of the day because something in his soul was making him feel very uneasy.

Chapter 20
Cancun, Mexico...

On the rooftop of a small building the sniper lay still as possible. He took slow deep breaths, as he prepared himself for the routine he had done so many times before. As he relaxed his body he took four more breaths, and slowly exhaled-clearing his mind in preparation. He settled his body flat on the roof and looked into the scope of his Remington 700. This weapon was designed to kill and he had the ultimate control over the trigger. He was one of the best snipers in the world.

As the all-white limo came to a stop, the door popped open and several armed men jumped out and started to access the scene before clearing the way. Moments later a Latin man with a dark complexion, and shoulder length flowing black hair stepped out the limo. The sniper slowly took in another breath and as he exhaled the cross-hairs were focused directly on the man's head. Without warning the sniper pulled the trigger and the impact of the mercury-tipped slug entered the man's head; exploding his brain on impact.

Immediately the bodyguards ran to shield the Latin man who was now lying on the ground; and they searched the scene for the trigger-man. The scene quickly became chaotic as passerby's started screaming as they realized a man was just killed in broad day light.

The sniper began to strip down his high-powered rifle and placed it securely in its case. As he put the case in an oversized black carrying bag, he made his way off the roof by climbing down an escape ladder that was located near the back of the building.

Once off the roof he entered a black Range Rover, where a short Dominican man had been in the driver's seat waiting on him. When the sniper got into the passenger seat, he pulled out his phone and placed a call.

"Did you take care of it Paul?"

"Yes, Mr. Watson, our problem in Mexico is no more. I'm on my way back to D.C. now."

Paul Warner closed his eyes as he hung up the phone and lay back in his seat. He had just killed another powerful drug King-Pin and terrorist for the U.S. Government. This is what he was known for. He killed without a trace and was better known as "The Eraser". Now the only man presently on his list was Norman "Face" Smith Jr.

Chapter 21
Hahnemann University Hospital...

For three days and two nights, Pamela lay in a coma barely clinging to life. The doctors had done all they could do and all that was left to do now was for everyone to wait it out. Veronica and Tasha never left the hospital, and even though Tasha suggested Veronica go home and get some rest because she had had a seizure, she stayed.

The detectives had visited the hospital and tried to get Veronica to tell them what she saw and if Pamela had said anything to her before coming into the hospital. Veronica was fully aware of who was responsible for shooting her best friend but the code of the street didn't change just because it had been Pamela. Quincy was the only person besides Veronica that knew Robbie had shot Pamela. Once she had told him he made her promise she wouldn't tell Tasha until Face had been informed.

Furthermore, Veronica didn't know how much Tasha knew about Robbie. She didn't know if Pamela or Face had told her that Robbie was the son Pamela regretted, the son she never wanted, and the son she could never love.

As the two women stood by Pamela's bed they tried their best to be strong because they knew she could hear them. Veronica had trouble keeping her tears back because just looking at the tube that was down her best friend's throat was killing her. She had never seen Pamela in this condition and Veronica could have never imagined this could possibly be the last place she'd see her best friend and sister.

Tasha looked over at Veronica and saw the tears falling from her face. She picked up a box of tissues and handed them to Veronica. "She's in so much pain Tasha…I just can't stand to see her like this." Tasha hugged Veronica and then held Pamela's hand. "God we come to you asking that you please let my mom recover. She is a strong woman but she needs your strength and courage to see her through this. I pray God that you please bring her out of this…"

Tasha had begun to tear up and wasn't able to finish the prayer. Veronica and Tasha just broke down and tried their best to maintain their composure. As Veronica began to walk out of the room to get some water, she noticed the hospital orderly who had been hanging around the room.

She looked up at him and said, "How can we help you." He quickly responded, "No, I'm just checking to see if you ladies need anything…water or tea, I could bring it to you." Veronica thanked him for his consideration but told him she needed to take a little walk and he moved on. Veronica had told Quincy about the orderly just as a precaution. He told her not to worry and that he would look into it, but she knew his main focus was on contacting Face.

Center City, Philadelphia…

"That bitch ain't dead yet!" Robbie yelled. " I shot her ass three times point blank range…I should have emptied the clip on her good for nothing ass." Arianna looked at her brother and said "Calm down Robbie. She's in a coma and there's a chance she

103

might die any day now. It's not like they have upgraded her condition or anything. She will die eventually, just calm down."

Arianna sat on the sofa and watched as her brother continued to pace the floor. Her words had no impact on him and he just appeared to grow angrier. Pamela clinging to life had not been the outcome he was looking for and for the past two days he had been unable to sleep.

"I should go to that damn hospital and put that bitch out of her misery. This time I will finish the job." Arianna was worried because she knew he might have been telling the truth and she didn't want Robbie to do anything in the current state he was in. "Listen Robbie, you have to calm down. You have made daddy proud and I know you're upset that your mother…" Robbie instantly interrupted her, "She's not my fuckin mother." Arianna corrected herself, "I know you're mad she's not dead but you have to calm down."

Robbie rushed towards the front door and Arianna thought about chasing after him but he needed time to cool off. Nothing she was saying to him was working and she didn't want to aggravate him anymore. He was now in a mind-set that she knew only he could control. If he wanted to rethink his next move, he would but the choice was his to make. She knew that for her brother's sake she had to be calm and meticulous. There was no use in both siblings acting irrational.

However, she knew Robbie was just like their father and when they exploded, their tempers spiked and patience lost out always.

Inside of the condo's parking lot Robbie got inside of his Mercedes and turned on the engine. Promptly the sounds of hardcore rap flowed out of the speakers and he turned the music up to the highest volume. As he sat back listening to the beat and lyrics of Tupac's Hail Mary, he quickly rolled up a blunt and lit it up. He had heard his sister and he knew he had to calm down, so he needed to smoke to bring himself down.

On the first inhale, he took a deep puff and let the marijuana fill his lungs as the drug made its way to his brain, before releasing a large cloud of smoke out of his nostrils. Robbie continued to smoke as he reached into his glove compartment. He took out a small photo of his deceased father and stared at the picture for a few moments.

"Don't worry dad I'm gonna get all of them for you. I'm gonna hurt everyone who is responsible for you and mom not being here anymore. They took your heart out dad...your fuckin heart!" As he continued to smoke his blunt, he let his tears fall and momentarily wash away his pain.

Chapter 22

Face and Reese sat inside of the limousine that was headed to an awaiting yacht. Their trip to the Bahamas had been a great success and turned out better than both could have imagined. Not only was their connect supplying them with enough cocaine to be distributed all across the East Coast but they had gotten their revenge on the Gomez brothers.

Face thought about the first time he had met the Gomez brothers and how linking up with them had gotten him secured financially. Not in a million years did he think they would testify against him. Now their betrayal had cost them their life and Face didn't have any more concerns with his old adversaries.

Face was now dedicated to his new connect and taking over new regions. He trusted that being loyal would keep him where he wanted to be and he had learned that from his mom early in life; loyalty was often all a man had and he'd never forget that lesson.

As Face looked over at Reese who was asleep in the limo, he knew he had a true friend and confidant in him. Reese had matured a bit but the old Reese was someone Face would always respect and love. He was a man who had served his time in prison without blaming or complaining, and now that he was out he was back on board to make moves and lots of money.

The clear blue ocean often brought a feeling of peace to Face but he was still feeling a little off. He tried to fight that feeling and a small smile came to his face, but it was quickly dissolved because he didn't feel right. He had no idea of the troubles waiting for him once he got back home to Philly, but his intuition was telling him something was up.

Northern Liberties...

Doc sat in the passenger's seat of Quincy's car as he waited for Quincy to come out of the house they had recently pulled in front of. As soon as Quincy returned to the car Doc didn't hesitate fulfilling his curiosity.

"Who was the woman at the door?" Quincy laughed and said, "Doc, she's a friend of mine." As he stared the car Doc continued, "Will I get a chance to taste her eyes?" Quincy couldn't believe what Doc had just said. He was feening for some eyeballs and Quincy gave him a look as if he needed to chill out. "Doc, she's a friend of mine alright but soon you'll have some eyeballs. Face will be back shortly and the list still has names on it so you'll get your treat...how can you even eat those things though?"

Doc was excited that someone was interested in his hobby but even more excited about the thought that he would soon be getting some new eyeballs. "Quincy, they're no different from eating snails or chocolate covered roaches. They have a different texture than your normal snack but they're delicious. They make me see better." Quincy stomach was turning as the thought about Doc eating the eyeballs. He didn't care what description Doc gave, he would never eat or taste an eyeball.

"Well I don't eat snails or roaches so you know I ain't eating no eyeballs." Doc laughed and said "Well that leaves more for me. I can't wait for Face to get back." As Doc smiled and appeared to be consumed with the thoughts of eating eyeballs, Quincy kept his eyes on the road and shook his head because Doc was and enigma and he'd never be able to understand him.

21st Street & Hunting Park Avenue
North Philly...

Detective Ron Perry sat inside of his car, directly across the street from the Lou & Choo's bar. He watched as a group of men stood around a long line of motorcycles, and he noticed they were all members of the notorious Ghost Ryder's motorcycle gang. With focused eyes, he scanned through the crowd as he searched for the individual he intended to meet up with. Upon making a visual contact, he beeped the horn and signaled the man, prompting him to leave the crowd and walk over to the car.

A short husky white man, who had tattoos all over his face and body, cautiously entered the car. "Damn man, what you trynna do...get me killed" he asked, looking over at Ron Perry.
"Calm the fuck down Mack, ain't nobody gonna fuck with you" Ron said.
"Yes the fuck they will. If they find out I'm an informant I'll have no chance to live my life. I'm one of the top leaders in my bike gang, you can't be showing up like this. You know they don't fuck with narks."
"Just let me know what's going on in the streets."

Mack was pissed. He knew he would have to give up answers but he wished Ron would have picked a better location. For over a year Mack had been one of Ron's unofficial employees and it was his job to give up information, but Mack didn't want to be exposed. For Mack's cooperation Ron allowed Mack and his gang to sell and distribute drugs through the city. Ron made sure he gave Mack a heads-up if any heat was coming his way, and he never interfered when Mack and the crew showed up on his radar.

"Well I heard Face had something to do with the F.B.I. agents' murders."

"Really, did you get that information from a reliable? source?"

"Of course I did or I wouldn't have told you. The streets know what's going on. Who else would be able to knock off two agents and their wives and go unnoticed?"

Ron Perry sat quiet for a minute.

"What else you got for me?"

"I heard that Face got a professional hit-man from Cali on his team. He goes by the name of Q. I heard he's a real low-key type of dude."

"What does he look like?"

"That I don't know. Nobody seems to know what he looks like. They just know the nigga name Q."

Mack was confused. Why was Ron worried about what moves Face was making?

"Ron, what's the deal on Face. You know he ain't the man no more. After the trial a lot of shit slowed up for him. What I hear is that he's outta the drug game and just trying to hold on to his real estate business."

"Don't believe everything you hear."

Mack got out of the car and went back to his crew. Ron Perry sat in his car for a minute thinking. He knew Face was never going to be out of the drug-game and that he was only waiting for Reese to get home for him to kick it into full gear. Ron Perry's motto was once a drug-dealer always a drug-dealer...especially once you've reach Kingpin status. For Face he knew the only thing that would end his reign was death.

Chapter 23
Three Days Later
Hahnemann University Hospital...

Since touching U.S. soil, Face had not left his mother's side. For three days he sat in a chair in his mother's room and watched her for hours. Tasha had to bring him clothes up to the hospital because he wasn't going to leave the hospital, even if it was to bathe and change his clothing.

Veronica told Face everything that she knew and when she informed him that Robbie was the shooter, Face was dumfounded. He couldn't believe his little brother tried to cut out his heart by taking Pamela away from him. The news hit him like a ton of bricks and he quickly let the streets know there was a $100,000 hit on Robbie's head. He offered an additional $50,000 to the person who brought him his head. All the love that Face once had for Robbie had faded because he had crossed the line. Robbie had now gone to the top of his list and had to be taken care of quickly.

As Face sat in the chair staring at his mother in her comatose state, Quincy walked into the room. He had gotten a call from Face to meet him at the hospital and he rushed over to see what was going on. "What's up Face, what's going on?"
Face asked Quincy to come closer and then he whispered into his ear. "I'm done waiting and playing games. I want all of them dead now. Peter, Watson, Ron Perry, Truck and Robbie. I want Robbie done right now."

Quincy had never heard Face speak in such a harsh and coarse tone. He could tell Face had been crying because his eyes were bloodshot red. His entire Face was consumed with worry and Quincy knew Pamela was his greatest love. The only thing that could possible soothe Face besides the death of his enemies, was for his mother to make a full recovery.

"I'm on it Face. Reese and I got your back, you just be here for mom's and we got you." Face stood up and gave Quincy a hug. He was hurting profoundly and he was starting to blame himself for this happening. He kept thinking that if only he had come back earlier from his trip, then this wouldn't have happened.

Before Face released Quincy from the hug, he again whispered in his ear "Kill them all. Their families and kids, I don't give a fuck, just kill them. If their friends love them kill them too." Face walked over to the hospital bed and grabbed his mother's hand. The tears formed and fell as he looked upon her swollen face. "Mom, I love you. Please, please don't die on me."

Villanova, PA...

Veronica, Tasha, and Passion sat around talking as the children ran around playing. Tasha watched as Lil Norman played with his younger sister Suri and Amiaya; Reese's four year old daughter. Tasha made the decision not to tell the children about their grandmother's current condition. The children shared a close bond with Pamela and she wasn't sure how the children would react to such horrific news; so when they asked where she was, Tasha lied and said their grandmother was on vacation. It hurt Tasha deeply to lie to her children but under the circumstances she didn't know what else to do.

All the women in their circle were in pain and knew the best thing they could do was be there for Pamela and each other. Pamela was like a mother figure to the ladies, including Veronica, and now they weren't sure if she would pull through. No one ever thought about her not being around and now things were all too real.

To complicate matters, Face refused to be around anyone but his mother. Hahnemann hospital had now become his new home. He didn't even want her to have visitors; he only wanted to be there for his mom and to deal with his emotional turmoil alone. Tasha respected his request and although it was tearing her up inside that she couldn't support her husband, she gave him his space.

At night when Veronica and Passion would go home, Tasha would be all alone with the children. She would call Face just to hear his voice and he was brief and often rushed her off the phone. Face didn't want to hurt his wife but at the moment he had nothing to give her. He didn't know what to say to her so she could understand what he was going through, and he didn't have the energy to try to explain it to her either. He was drained and often left Tasha feeling empty and alone.

Tasha loved Face deeply and just wanted to be there for him. What he didn't understand was that

Tasha too was grieving and needed someone to be there for her. This was the side of Face, the cold and distant side she couldn't understand and didn't want to see.

Center City...

A block away from the Gallery Mall at 9th and Market Streets, Quincy pulled up on a small back street and parked his car. Reese was parked in the car in front of him. Quincy quickly got out and walked over to Reese's vehicle. When he rolled the window down Quincy said,

"It's a go. Face wants it done now."

"Okay, we can roll out to DC in another hour. Get all the men ready. Did you talk to Mike?"

"Yeah, he's waiting on us to get to D.C. now. He said everything is ready."

"Meet me at the safe house in an hour so we can roll out together" Reese said, before rolling up the tinted windows.

Quincy watched as Reese pulled off down the street. When he got in to his car a smile appeared on his face, because he couldn't wait to retaliate on the people that had done Face wrong.

It wasn't long before Quincy pulled up to one of their stash houses in Uptown. When he entered the car he went through the large arsenal of guns and ammunition, and began to choose what weapons he'd be taking with him to D.C.

Early The Next Morning
Washington, D.C...

Inside a large conference room at an undisclosed location, U.S. Senator C.W. Watson was surrounded by some of the most powerful men and women in America. Seated at the long oval table were the Vice President, The Secretary of State, The U.S. Attorney General and Senators and Congressman from seven of the largest states in the country. Everyone inside the room had a gold ring on their right index finger with a diamond-like symbol incrusted in the middle. They were secretly known as the C.O.U.P. The Committee of Unlimited Power.

Watson listened as the Attorney General spoke about the severe drug problems that were plaguing the United States and how many of those issues were steaming from the Mexican drug lords. "Our Border Control can't seem to keep these thugs out of our country! The Columbians are supplying the Mexicans and the Mexicans are using their resource to flood not only our ghettos, but they are getting it to our suburbs. Affluent children are overdosing at alarming rates. They must be stopped!"

The Attorney General paused as he pulled out a piece of paper that was inside of a folder in front of where he was seated. "This piece of paper contains confident information about the top drug-lord in the world. He is ten times bigger than Pablo Escobar and Fabio Ochoa Vásquez. His name is Roberto Fuentes and it's been confirmed that Mr. Fuentes is now the leader of the Los Rastrojos Cartel. I don't think I have to tell you guys how big that Cartel is but I'll

115

just reiterate that they are the largest supplier of drugs in all of Columbia. They also distribute drugs to a wide range of Mexican syndicates, including the powerful and dangerous Sinaloa Cartel."

The Attorney General paced the floor for a minute and said "The drugs and the violence has to stop! Our sources recently told us that Mr. Fuentes had a meeting down in the Bahamas just a few days ago, and Jose and Rico Gomez were in attendance. Those guys are on the top of the C.I.A. and F.B.I.'s most wanted list. There was also word that two other men were seen with them. Their identities have yet to be confirmed but what our sources tell us is that they were black males, and not from any Mexican or Columbian Cartel."

C.W. Watson stood up from his seat and said, "Everyone knows how I feel about these low-life scumbags. I will not allow them to rob our country of our innocence. I'm willing to do what I have to do to rid these thugs from our country." Watson was fuming and filed with anger. The one thing he hated more than anything in the world were drug-dealers; and everyone in the room knew it. "Does the committee agree?" Everyone stood up from their seats and raised their right hands in unison.

Chapter 24
Hahnemann University Hospital...

Tasha and Face were seated inside one of the hospital's private family visitation room, which was directly across the hall from Pamela's room. Face would go into that room when he wanted to talk on the phone or meet with Quincy because he didn't want to disturb his mom. That was the only place he would go because he was afraid to leave his mother's side. Face was not about to let anyone come up to the hospital and hurt her again.

Tasha had come up to the hospital to bring her husband some food and clothing, and to check on him. He was not himself and she was very worried about him.

"Why won't you let me be here for you?"

"Tasha please stop it. You are here for me I get that."

"No, you stop it. You don't want me here but she's my mother too. I guess you forgot that. I'm hurting too and I need you too."

"I just need some time alone...my mom is in a fuckin coma Tasha. Do you understand that? I don't know if she's going to die, shit the doctors can't even tell me what's going on with her! I need time to myself, please understand my mind is in a million pieces right now; I can't think straight."

"I know you're all over the place but I just want to be there for you, for us."

Face fell into Tasha arms and said "I'm sorry baby, you know I'll always need you and I love you...I'm sorry." He was weak and tired of the pain he was carrying. He just wanted his mother to wake up or show him a sign that she would get better. Pamela's wounds were serious and part of her stomach had to be removed because it was so badly damaged by the bullets. She had lost a great deal of weight in a short time, and was being fed through a feeding tube. Her stomach had not healed and doctors were greatly afraid she would catch an infection; so they cleaned her wounds often and everyone who visited had to wash their hands each time they entered and reentered the room.

When Tasha looked over at Pamela's room she noticed the hospital orderly that had been constantly monitoring the room. She told Face to slowly turn around and watch how he was gawking at his mother. Face quickly swung open the visitor room door and when he did, the orderly rushed down the hall. Face wasn't about to let him get away because there was no reason this guy would have been taking such an interest in his mother.

"Yo, hold up" Face said, as he grabbed the orderly by the back of his shirt. The orderly was trying his hardest to break away but Face had a firm grip. "Hey man, I work here" he said, panicking. The orderly knew who Face was and what he was capable of doing to him. "Motherfucka don't let me ask you again, who the fuck are you?" He was petrified and didn't want to blow his cover but he was hoping that he could at least keep his life. "I do work in the hospital but I work for Ron Perry too and he asked me to keep an eye out on your mother's condition." Face was fuming as he said, "Ron Perry, the detective right?" The orderly agreed.

Face saw a janitor's closet and walked into the closet with the orderly. "Please don't kill me" the man begged. "Shut the fuck up" Face said, as he looked at the man's ID tag on his shirt. "Vincent Jackson huh?" Vincent was stunned because he knew that he too had a family and know that Face knew his identity he didn't know what would happen to him. "Please Face, I have a wife and two children. I was just doing a job for Ron. He said it was official police work, I didn't know if he was protecting your mom or what." Face was disgusted with him but knew he was going to use this rat for all he knew. "Your wife and children will be dead in less than twenty-four hours unless you tell me everything you know and exactly what Ron wanted from you."

As Face loosened the grip around Vincent's neck, he said "Start talking."

Center City...

The rain was pouring down and ferociously smacking the windows in Arianna's condo. The thunder was loud and echoed from the heavens as Arianna stood by the window and stared at the greyish dark sky. The soulful sounds of Alicia Keys flowed from the speakers as Robbie was asleep on the sofa; stretched out as if he had no cares but his hand was clutched to his handgun.

Arianna couldn't sleep, so she had turned to one of her habitual hobbies; Googling Face on the Internet. She had a feeling like she had reached a dead-end because she wanted to know intimate details about Face. He was the man who would have to pay for murdering her parents but she had questions that she wanted him to answer.

Trying to find something to help her sleep, she exited her Internet search and went into the bathroom. She opened the medicine cabinet and took out a small container of pills. Arianna had been prescribed Zoloft to help her deal with the depression she lived with, and often when she took her pills she could rest better. The pills were a source of embarrassment for her because she couldn't fully control her suicidal thoughts or handle the depression. She struggled with therapy so her psychologist suggested she take Zoloft until she got to a place where she could better handle all the trauma and stress in her life.

Arianna was a beautiful woman who had an exotic beauty but her soul suffered and it was tainted. There was nothing but turmoil and pain flowing through her veins and she never paid attention to the men who would complement her beauty or ask her out. Her mind was not focused on dating when she often had to deal with her demons and control her suicidal urges.

As she sat down on the toilet, she took one of the pills and swallowed it. She closed her eyes and sat down on the bathroom floor. She was so tired of the pain she held inside. The day had to come when Face was gone and then she could live a carefree life, and only then she wouldn't have to deal with suicidal thoughts or take pills for depression. This is what she told herself as the tears flowed and a flash of lightning illuminated the bathroom.

West Philly…

Doc stood at the corner of 45th & Lancaster Avenue watching the female crossing-guard assists the children across the street. He had been watching her for weeks and loved seeing her. He knew what time she got to work and what time she got off. The thirst for a fresh kill had reached the boiling point for Doc; he couldn't go another day without killing someone. He was convinced that if he murdered someone it would calm all his rages and keep him content for a while.

As the rain made a free-fall to the earth, he watched the woman with murder drawn in his eyes. The rain pouncing on his face didn't bother him and he was holding a large syringe inside his hand. The crossing-guard safely walked another group of children across the street, and she watched them in the distance as they made their way home. She loved her job and was always happy. She was so concerned with the children that she didn't see the weird looking, older white man approach her.

"Blue is my favorite color."

"Excuse me?" the crossing guard asked, stunned to see him standing there.

"I said your eyes are perfect."

"Perfect for what" she asked, feeling creped out.

"For eating" Doc said, as he quickly stabbed the syringe into the woman's neck.

The ordeal happened so quickly. She hadn't even had a chance to scream because the potency of the medication in the syringe made her fall into Doc's arms without a struggle. No one was around and Doc swept up his victim and carried her down the street. With the rain providing the perfect cover he got away unnoticed.

Ten minutes later Doc had taken the women through an alley that led to his small row-home. He held the woman tightly in his arms, as he led her into the dungeon of hell. Once in the basement, Doc laid her across a long wooden table. He then began to remove his raincoat before getting back to his victim.

Today Doc wanted something different. He still would enjoy his eyeball treats but he wanted some sex. He prided himself on being a great lover and when he was done he'd enjoy some time in bed watching the latest episode of CSI.

Chapter 25
Hahnemann University Hospital...

"I swear to you, that's all I know. Ron Perry wanted
  me to tell him who was coming to see your mom.
  He always wanted to know if you came through and
  he always called to see if she...I mean your mom's
  condition had gotten worse."
"So where will he be next Saturday?"
"He's going to be at the North American Inn Motor
  on City Line Avenue. They have a ballroom there
  and it's his 25th anniversary party."
"And you're sure he'll be there?"
"Yes, he's going to be there for sure. He's really
  excited about it. I could hear it in his voice. Plus he
  said if anything happens on Saturday and I can't
  reach him, it's because he's at his anniversary
  party."
"Vincent, don't bullshit me. Everybody you love,
  their lives depend on it.
"No Sir, I swear to you that I'm telling you the truth.
  He'll be there for sure.

Face had gotten the information he needed to
deal with Ron Perry. This guy had killed Momma
and DJ and thought he could keep tabs on Face and
his mother. He wasn't going to have much time to
enjoy his party Face, thought to himself.

Before leaving the janitor's closet, Face had
called Quincy and gotten the location of Vincent's
home, the daycare his children went to and the job his
wife worked at. Face wanted Vincent Jackson to
know that he wasn't messing with some small time
fool and that if he had gave up the wrong information

or tried to alert Ron Perry, he had just exterminated his entire family.

"I just want us to be clear. You don't speak a word of this to Ron. Just keep telling him what you've been telling him but let him know my mom's condition has gotten worse and that it doesn't seem like she'll make it."

Face didn't like the taste of his words as they came out his mouth but he knew Ron wanted his mother dead. He wanted Ron to feel comfortable and ease up a bit because he was surely going to be caught off guard.

"My lips are sealed and I'll do just as you say. Please just don't kill me or my family."

"I won't...you have my word."

Chapter 26
Chestnut Hill...

Inside of Veronica's beautiful and tranquil home, her naked body laid across the silky sheets as they caressed her body. Her face was deeply pressed into the soft, plush pillow, and the rain dancing on her window pane relaxed her body. She was drained from a night of intense and aggressive lovemaking with her new lover Carter.

Veronica slowly pulled herself from the comforts of her bed and sat on the edge. Carter was in the bathroom talking on his cellphone, and as Veronica placed on her silk robe she slyly walked to the bathroom door. She listened deeply and was shocked at what she had just heard.

Fear surged throughout her body as she tiptoed back into her bedroom. She quickly reached under her mattress and pulled out a loaded 9mm, which she had always kept there for protection.

As Carter exited the bathroom he walked into the bedroom but was stopped dead in his tracks. His eyes grew wide as he was now staring at Veronica, who had her gun pointed directly at him.
"What the hell is going on?"
"No, who the fuck do you work for?"

Carter looked at Veronica but she wasn't the same woman who he had spent countless nights fucking. She was serious and ready to make a move.
"Okay, calm down Veronica. I really need you to put that gun away."
"Yeah, you would like that but that's not what's going to happen. You better start answering

questions if you want to get home to your wife."

"I work for a special unit that's ran by the government."

" A special unit? Who, the F.B.I. or the C.I.A.?"

"No, the unit is a private division with more power and fewer restrictions on what we can do."

"I see, because fucking me is definitely not something the F.B.I. would have condoned. So what were you sent here to do?"

"I'd rather not say" he said, feeling unsure if she had the guts to pull the trigger.

Veronica aimed the gun at his dick.

"I don't think you have a choice in the matter. Who are you working for and what did you come here to do?"

"The Vice President is my boss and I'm working for C.W. Watson and a man that goes by the name The Eraser."

"So Watson put you up to this?"

After a long sigh he responded.

"Veronica a lot of people want you dead, very important and powerful people."

"You want me dead too…"

"No, I'm just doing my job. It's nothing personal just my job."

"So you were supposed to get the tapes and then what?"

"Watson wants the tapes because he said they will ruin his political career. He can't have those tapes out here. He can't have those tapes controlling his destiny."

The room was silent. Veronica was sick and thinking how she could have been killed by Carter for the tapes. Pamela had warned her, Face had warned her, and she knew she couldn't trust anyone. How could she have been so sloppy?

"How long have you been assigned to me?"

"It's been a three year process."

"A process?"

"Yes, we had to do surveillance and sometimes wiretaps."

"You fucks have been watching me for three damn years. I can't believe this shit. Oh, and who gave you the money to pay me…Watson?"

"Yes."

"Carter, those tapes have many homes. They will never disappear and if anything happens to me, they'll be distributed to all media outlets and the cat will be out of the bag."

"We understand that, that's why…"

"That's why what!"

"That's why he's going to kill those you have given the tapes to. He can't risk letting the tapes get out."

"You have a lot to say now. Why are you just telling me this?"

"Veronica, you have a gun pointed at me…I have no other choice but to talk. I don't want to die, that's outside of my pay scale."

Veronica felt so betrayed and maybe she only had herself to blame. She had gotten emotionally connected to Carter even though she had told herself she hadn't. It was something she just couldn't control. All this time she had been sleeping with the enemy and she had been nothing more to him than a job; one where someone paid him to follow her around and to fuck her. She felt cheap, she felt dirty and a sickening feeling had exploded inside her stomach.

"Veronica if you give up those tapes, he won't hurt you, or Face or Pamela. All they want are the tapes. Don't get yourself caught up in all this mess over some tapes. These are powerful men who will stop at nothing and you are too beautiful for all this. Just give up the tapes, all of them."

"No, if I give up those tapes they'll kill me anyway. Whether you get the tapes or not, you were going to kill me."

"No, I...I wasn't."

"Save it you fucking bastard. You mean to tell me you were fucking me and just going to kill me like I was a nobody."

"No, last night was about more than my job. I've come to really care for you. I was begging them to let you out of this as soon as you gave up the tapes. They are not going to bother you as soon as you give them the tapes."

"That's what's wrong with you...you're a horrible fuckin liar. The tapes were not going to save my life and I don't see why your fucked up lies should save yours."

Veronica lifted the gun up and pointed it at his chest, then she fired it twice. As the bullets hit him in the chest, he stumbled before falling to the ground. "Bitch you fucking shot me" he said, holding his chest and looking at the blood that was flowing from his wounds. "Fuck you Carter" as she began walking towards his body. "They are going to kill you bitch. All of you fucks are going to die." She stood over his body and smiled, "Maybe so, but today I'm going to kill you" she said, as she emptied the remaining bullets into his body.

She rushed to her closet and got out a cellphone that she was only to use in case of emergencies. Once she dialed the number, it rang three times before it was answered.

"What's up Veronica?"

"Face I need you to get to my house now."

"Right now, you know I'm with my mom."

"Right now Face!"

"Okay, I'm on my way."

Veronica went into the living room and sat on her couch. She had never been this scared and she could barely keep her legs from shaking. There was a dead government agent in her bedroom and she didn't know what that meant. Were there people outside watching her home, would they rush into her home and kill her? She didn't know what to think or what to do. In that moment she cried and prayed to God for protection. As the thunder struck, she was startled and wished that Face would get there very soon.

Chapter 27
Hahnemann University Hospital...

Inside of a tinted black Lexus that was borrowed from his cousin, Truck was parked directly across the street from the hospital. He had been in the car for the past two days and he only got out when he had to feed the meter, grab something quick to eat, or use the bathroom. He had been waiting to see Face and although he hadn't seen him yet, he was sure Face was inside the hospital with his mother. The bond the two shared had been strong ever since he had known the two; they were inseparable, and so he knew Face was inside. He had watched and saw Tasha come in and out but still he had no visual on Face.

Truck needed to get some things off of his chest. He knew what he had done and he was eager to explain it all to Face. His conscious had been eating him up and there was no way he could deal with this any longer. He couldn't live his life on the run and he had to deal with whatever was going to come his way. So for now, he had to sit and wait.

Later That Evening...

The trip to D.C. had taken Reese, Quincy, and their men a little over three hours for them to arrive. Reese and Quincy rode together while the other men followed behind in a black tinted van. The men all adorned serious expressions because Face had sent a message clear and strong, that now was the time to cut off some heads.

On the corner of Minnesota Avenue, Reese and Quincy met up with Mike Conway. He had been on his job and had done great work with collecting the information they would need to make their move a success. There was nothing that Mike didn't know about the men he tailed and he was certain they would be well informed for whatever they had in store for their targets.

"Okay y'all got it from here on out" Mike said, as he shook the men's hands and took the envelope that Quincy handed him. He had been paid for a job well done and knew his part of the mission was over. "Thanks Mike, we got it from here" Quincy said, as Mike got in his car and pulled off in the darkness of the night.

Reese and Quincy were ready to handle business and there wasn't much more that needed to be said. As the two got into their car they looked at each other knowing that soon scores would be settled. Too many games had been played and they were no longer in the arcade business. They were tired of men with titles thinking they had real power, because they were about to show them exactly what labels meant to people who wouldn't hesitate to eliminate them from the equation. They were not in D.C. for a drill; the men had come to clean house.

Chestnut Hill, PA...

Face stood over the dead agent and just shook his head. He had no care for him but he was disgusted at how far Watson and his men would go. He walked over to Carter's jeans and searched his pants for his wallet. Once he found it he took out his identification and looked for identifiable information. Carter's real name was Larry Sickler and he was thirty years old, with a New York City driver's license. He also got his cellphone out of his pockets and then headed downstairs.

Veronica was still badly shaken up and had since had a few shots of Southern Comfort to ease the shakes she had developed. Face had one of his men on the front door, and two watching the house from inside the car. It was a slight relief to Veronica but she was so messed up she didn't know if she'd ever be okay.

"Face, what I am going to do" she asked, because she was scared out of her wits. "Don't worry Veronica I'll take care of everything. You said no one knew he was here today right?" Veronica wished she could say for sure but he was on the phone in the bathroom and things had been said. "That's what he told me but I overheard him in the bathroom mentioning Pam." Face was annoyed and puzzled as he said, "My mother...how did he know about my mom?"

It was true, she had made a mistake but now it was time to fess up because being dishonest could make matters much worse. "Face I fucked up. I got caught up and when Pam got hurt...he was there for me. I mean, I didn't know he was going to be some agent and shit, I just wanted to talk to someone about what I was feeling. I'm sorry...really, I am so sorry."

Veronica began to cry as she realized she had gone against her better judgment in a moment of weakness. She was a smart woman and had always played by the rules, but with Carter, he had gotten into her head and definitely into her heart. She allowed herself to be vulnerable and that was the one thing she hated. For Veronica she always wanted to be in control; having power over her clients was her pleasure fix.

"Don't cry and don't fuck up like that again…your tricks should just be your toys and you know that. I have someone outside that's gonna take you to my house in Bala Cynwyd and he'll stay with you while you're there. Get your things together and get rid of that cellphone…I'll get you another one."

Veronica was pleased that Face didn't go off on her. She never wanted to hurt him and there wasn't anything she wouldn't do to see him happy and living the life he always wanted. Face was pained to see Veronica cry and he didn't want to see her hurt; and although he was upset with her, he knew that she was family, and had been hurting just like he was. He understood that sometimes people speak when they just shouldn't.

Face gave Veronica a comforting hug and kissed her on the cheek, and then she gathered some of her belongings. He walked her to the car and told his man to take care of her, and then he walked back into the house. There was a body to get rid of, a crime scene to clean up, and Face knew Larry Sickler's employer would soon be looking for him.

Chapter 28
Washington, D.C...

Paul Warner walked into C.W. Watson's office and sat down at the empty chair. Watson was happy to see his buddy and anxious to find out about his trip.

"How was Mexico" Watson asked with a devilish grin.

"Mexico was great. Got rid of another wetback scumbag...so I'll say it was a trip worth taking."

"Wonderful job Paul, wonderful job indeed."

"Anything for the red, white and blue."

"Paul you're a true American hero. If we don't clean up this country soon the niggers, Jews, and Mexicans will take it over! The Committee needs more good men like yourself."

"Don't you worry boss, every time one of them gets too big for their britches just call on me. You know I'll knock them down a peg or just wipe them out."

"So, what did you need to speak to me about", Watson asked, searching for his cigar.

"Peter Greenberg."

"What about him? We already took him for a billion dollars and he's scared to death right now."

"I want him dead...after we get his password and personal info to his offshore accounts. He changed the password so we'll have to get the new one but after that he's of no use to anyone."

Watson sat there contemplating what Paul was saying. Why did he want to make such a move when he'd just become a wealthy man? He had five hundred million and that was more than most men would ever see in their lives. He had lit his cigar and began to smoke it.

"And when would you like this done?"

"To tell you the truth now's a good time. We have no use for this guy. He's a fucking thief and tonight my schedules looks clear."

Watson stood up from his chair as he thought about what Paul was saying.

"Paul I have no problem with that. Just make sure you get the current password before you get rid of him. That son-of-a-bitch has over five billion dollars and I would be very upset if that money didn't become ours."

"I'll get it. That sick fuck never made an honest dollar in his life. He's like those damn Jews and I wish the Germans would have gotten rid of all of them."

"Calm down my friend. We have to remain calm and take care of the business at hand. Just make sure our mess is gone and no one is the wiser."

"Don't worry Sir, I've got it all covered."

"Oh, how are things in Philadelphia?"

"We'll have those tapes real soon. My guy has that black whore wrapped around his dirty little finger. She'll do anything for him soon enough."

Both men laughed as they pictured the freaky and nasty acts Veronica and Larry had indulged in.

"Great because those tapes are of the highest priority."

"Understood. I talked to him earlier and he told me he was in New York doing some shopping or something; but things are moving in the right direction. He said he'd be back in D.C. tomorrow to

debrief me. Also, something has happened with
Face's mother…something about her being shot."
"What, really?"
"That's what he told me. I'm sure he'll give me all
the details tomorrow."
"Great, for now let's stay focused on the money and
getting rid of that thieving Jew" Watson said, as
the grin of greed appeared upon his face.

West Philadelphia

Lying on Doc's bed was a female's corpse,
which was stiff and cold. Hours earlier he had slit her
throat and wrist and there was nothing she could do,
because the injection she had received left her
cataleptic. Doc watched joyously as she bled out and
seeing her blood paint the sheets gave him a hard-on.
But just watching wasn't enough for Doc.
Naked and erect he covered himself in his victim's
blood. His dick look like a candy-cane and he began
to sodomize her as he became overwhelmed with his
urges to penetrate his corpse. When he was done with
his anal torment, he flipped her over and spread her
legs far apart. Without hesitation he grabbed her hips
and thrust his dick into her lifeless vagina; pounding
away at it. He was so into the act you would have
thought the woman was alive and begging him for
more.
It took Doc only a few minutes to reach his
climax and once he ejaculated, he cuddled next to his
victim and grabbed the remote control. He cut on the
TV and flipped through the channels until he got to
his favorite, CSI. He turned to his friend and said

"Don't say a word, this is my favorite show. We can get back to business once it goes off." Then he kissed her on the lips and began to watch his beloved program.

Chestnut Hill, PA...

All evidence of Agent Sickler had been removed. It was as if he had never visited Veronica's home and that's exactly how Face needed it to appear. His body was bagged up and sent to a crematory; which Face had used many other times. The only items that remained where the agent's ID, cellphone-which was checked for a tracking device-and the Glock Face found in his leather jacket. By now it was apparent to him that no one was scooping out Veronica's home because no one made any attempt to reach him and no one was knocking at the door. He had a feeling that Agent Sickler may have been at her home for a personal visit and his lust had cost him his life.

Veronica was stashed away at his home in Bala Cynwyd and he knew she would be safe there. The security systems on his home were top-notch and he had one of his best men guarding her as well. He had no physical ties to the home because one of his lawyers had it deeded to a fake company whose owner was merely a ghost. With everyone in their place Face made his way back to the hospital to be with his mother. He had hired security to keep watch over her but still he never felt comfortable unless he was on duty.

Chapter 29
Washington, D.C...

The stars illuminated the pitch black skies. At the end of the block there was a black tinted van parked, and Face's most loyal and trusted men were armed and inside of the car. Directly situated on the opposite side of the street was Quincy and Reese, both disguised as two homeless bums. Underneath their tattered and loose clothing, Reese and Quincy had their .45's-with silencers attached-gripped and in hand. The plan was to get it done quickly and get out even quicker; leaving no witnesses.

Patiently they had been awaiting Peter's arrival and according to Mike the late night jog would take place at approximately 9:30 pm. At present it was 9:23 pm and so far no one had seen Peter J. Greenberg. Each moment that passed seemed as if time had slowed or possibly paused. One of the worst things about doing a hit was waiting to do the hit.

At 9:30 pm Quincy tapped Reese because he had spotted Peter and two large men walking towards them. The men in the car who were watching the scene from their night-vision binoculars were given the signal to be ready; and they responded by sending a text message to the designated cell phone in Quincy's pocket that began to vibrate.

Reese was seated on the ground, as he held a bottle of cheap beer in his left hand, and under his coat he gripped his weapon. An enemy of Face was an enemy to him and the family, so this day was long overdue. When Peter and his two bodyguards got closer, Quincy, who was limping, approached them.

"Excuse me Sir, but can you spare some change for a guy who's down on his luck." Peter was not about to waste his time helping anyone, especially after the ordeal he was going through. "Get out of my face and go find a job, you damn bum" he said, as one of his bodyguards pushed Quincy away. Quincy struggled a bit and the other bodyguard said "Move it you bum, didn't you hear the guy. No one's giving you any change." Quincy responded saying "Sir, I'm a Gulf war Vet, can you just spare a quarter?"

The bodyguard who has just reiterated that he needed to leave now had gotten a soft spot. "You are, I'm one too. Man I'm sorry about that let me see what I got." When he looked up to hand Quincy the change he had gathered from his pockets, he was surprised to see a .45 being aimed at his Face. THHHHTTT....two bullets silently entered his skull and he stumbled before falling to the ground.

After hearing a thump, Peter and the other bodyguard quickly turned around to see what was going on. Seeing his partner lying on the ground, he quickly tried to reach for his weapon but before he could make a move Reese had sent a slug deep into the back of his head. It was an instant kill and had sent pieces of brain matter flying onto the sidewalk.

Peter was quickly gripped up by Quincy. "Say one fucking word and your next mothafucker." He had just saw that the men were not in the mood for negotiations, so he shut up and when the black tinted van pulled up he was ushered in without resistance.

As the van drove towards their next destination, Peter sat quiet and terrified. He had paid Watson and Paul a whole lot of money and not one dime of it had helped him escape his impending fate. One of the men in the van duck tapped Peter's mouth and handcuffed him. He didn't know who was responsible for his kidnapping because he had so many enemies. He was a wanted many in many countries. The Russians, Chinese and Columbians all had bounty's on his head.

Peter was shaking and he didn't know if he'd be able to buy or talk his way out of this. His mind was racing and he tried to eliminate his enemies to see if he could figure out who was responsible for his abduction. He kept thinking it had to be the Russians because they'd crossed boundaries to get their men; and they had no problem with killing anyone who stood in their way. Peter was worried and he knew the man responsible for his life was not in the van because no one said a word as the van sped on. He had fucked up, he thought. The manipulation and theft had gotten out of control. He was in too deep but he badly wanted out.

The dark-blue Dodge Magnum driving closely behind the van was occupied by Reese and Quincy. "We got Peter" Reese said to Face. "Good, take care of that other problem and I'll meet y'all at Doc's later tonight." Something was a bit off in their conversation and although everything seemed to be okay, Reese still needed to ask. "Hey, is everything cool." Face who under normal circumstances would have celebrated Peter's capture was not in the mood. "Man, I'm pissed. I'm looking at my mom in this coma and…I can't stand this much longer. She's gotta wake up. She's in a fuckin coma man. My mom's in the hospital in a fuckin coma."

Face needed to vent and Reese didn't have any problems listening. He knew how it felt to lose someone close and after losing Momma and DJ, he had literally felt his heart break. He was hopeful that Pamela would pull out of her coma but for now he knew Face would have many emotions that he wouldn't' be able to control.

"I love you man, I'll see you soon and I need you to hang in there. You know I know how you're feeling and we still got her. We have to fight for her…we ain't giving up and neither is she." The words were a momentary comfort for Face and he was relieved to have someone to confide in. "Oh, some shit came up with Veronica but I'll talk to you about that when we meet up. Talk to you later."

Quincy, who had overheard the phone conversation, understood what was going on. He was going to do everything in his power to help Face lighten his load. "The list has gotten shorter" he said to Reese. "Yeah but we got a lot more names to go" he said, looking at Quincy. "True. I feel sorry for Peter. Shit, I don't even want to know what's going to happen to that dude." Reese laughed and said "Fuck all of them. Watson, the Gomez brothers, and everybody else who's crossed our brother. Death is all they deserve and once they get it I hope they all take a trip to hell." Quincy nodded his head as he sipped on his Pepsi and continued to drive to their next destination.

Chapter 30

Face made his way pass his mother's hospital bed and stood in front of the large window. He stared out of the window and thought of the many things that had happened in his life. For years he had been strategically masterminding his plots for revenge. C.W. Watson, Peter J. Greenberg and The Gomez Brothers have all been at the top of his list. Peter was captured but he could not delight in his capture.

Now, as he stared out of the window at the dark sky all he could think about was his mother's current condition. Doctors had told him there was nothing more they could do. There was no amount of money that he could pay to have his mom fixed; it was now in God's hands. As he turned away from the window his emotions had made their way onto his cheeks. His tears felt like burning acid and as he wiped away his tears, he walked back to his mom's bedside. He stood over her hoping she would say his name or reach for him. His eyes welled up with tears and his mind drifted away to another time and place.

1987
Philadelphia, PA...

When Pamela walked through the front door Momma was sitting on the sofa with Reese and DJ; watching her daytime soap-*The Young & The Restless*.

"How is he doing" Pamela asked, as she removed her coat. "He still has a high fever. I gave him his meds and fed'em some soup, but you know the only thing that will make him feel better is his mother" Momma said. "It's only been a day...I had to make an important run. Momma hushed her away because she was into her stories "Go on to your boy, that childs upstairs in that bed waiting on you."

Pamela knew Momma was serious about those stories, and after saying hello to the boys she headed upstairs. When she walked into the bedroom Face was laying under the overs. She rushed over to him and sat beside him.

"Hey baby, how you feeling?" Even though he was sick, the huge smile that was on his face let her know he had missed her and would be okay. "I feel better but Momma thinks I'm too sick to get out of bed." She smiled and soothing said "Listen to Momma. She only wants the best for you and trust me; she knows your body needs to rest." Face was happy that his mom was back and didn't care if he had to stay in bed, as long as his mom was around. "I will listen to her but can you stay here with me, please?"

Pamela looked at her handsome seven year old son and a tear fell from her eye. She loved her son so much and she'd do anything to make him happy. "Yes baby, I'll stay." Face sat up and gave his mom a big hug. "Thank you mom, I promise I'll stay in bed until I get better." Pamela was pleased and said "And I promise you I'll stay by your side until you feel better."

Robbie quickly ran into the condo and shut the door behind him. "What's wrong" Arianna asked, as she jumped up from the sofa. Robbie walked over to the window and peeped out the curtains. "What's wrong Robbie" she asked again, now clearly frightened but he said nothing. He kept looking through the curtains as he clutched his gun in his right hand. "Robbie what's wrong...You're scaring the shit out of me" she said.

Robbie saw a car parked across the street and then moments later he watched as it pulled off and disappeared into the darkness. "Robbie what is going on" she demanded. He was frightened and had to make sure whoever was following him wasn't trying to get into their building. "Someone was following me." Arianna thought that he might be paranoid because of what he had done, so she asked "Are you sure?" He couldn't say for sure but he was sure. He wasn't going to go against his gut feeling. "Yes, I feel sure. It was someone inside of a black Honda following me for about three blocks. Then it parked and just pulled off."

Arianna reached out to hug her brother. This was serious and she didn't want anything to happen to Robbie, but he had been acting weird lately. "Robbie, try to calm down. Ever since you shot your mot...Pamela, you've been a nervous wreck." Robbie was a bit agitated by his sister's comments. He knew he was being followed. "Yeah but this time, this time I was being followed." Robbie walked back to the curtains to peep out and see if the black Honda had come back.

"I'm not stupid. I know Face has someone following me." Arianna shook her head. What if it was true? What were they going to do to her brother? "Let them come though...I'll kill all of them. I'm not scared of Face or none of his goons. I'm Hood Jr." Robbie said, but he didn't sound so convincing; especially since he almost broke his neck running into the house.

Arianna told her brother she'd be right back, and then walked down the hallway to the bathroom. Once inside she closed the door behind her and let out a long hard sigh. She stared into the mirror and then looked into her eyes. They were filled with tears and had become overcome with pain. As she stared she could hear Robbie yell out in the background "Come on Face, I'm ready motherfucker!"

Arianna opened the medicine cabinet and took out her anxiety pills that were sitting next to her depression medication. She noticed two were missing and as she quickly swallowed two pills down her throat. She realized Robbie must have taken her pills because occasionally he'd take her pills to calm himself down. She thought about swallowing all the pills in the bathroom but instead she sat on the toilet and waited for the effects of her meds to kick in; while she prayed and asked God to protect her brother.

Chapter 31
Silver Springs, Maryland...

The black tinted van parked about a mile away from C.W. Watson's luxurious home. The large house was surrounded by trees and beautiful landscape, and it was well hidden from passersby's. Reese, Quincy, and three of their best men were all dressed in camouflage outerwear. The place had been scouted and everything they needed to know about Watson had been learned; down to every possible escape route should they need to make a quick get-away from his home.

The men surrounded the house and made their way to their designated entryway. Through the night vision goggles they could see Watson in the living room talking to another man, and his wife was in the kitchen cooking on the stovetop. Quincy softly spoke into his walkie-talkie and said "its 10:45 fellas, five more minutes." Once he put his walkie-talkie inside his pocket he took out a live hand grenade.

Inside The Home of C.W. Watson...

"What the hell do you mean someone kidnapped Peter!"
"Watson I'm telling you someone took him and two of our best men were found dead on the street. One of them had his damn brains blown out."
"What the hell is going on" Watson fumed.
"I don't know but something is up and I'm going to get to the bottom of this. I can't even get in touch with Agent Sickler and that's not sitting well with

me. I've been calling and I get no answer, and he doesn't call back. Something very strange is up."
"We need to find out who is responsible for taking Peter and get him the fuck back."
"Maybe it was the Russians. Peter has stolen from so many people we can't keep up with his enemies."
"I don't give a damn who it was, we just have to get him back. No one steals for me!"

Watson was fuming and both he and Paul were in total disbelief. Who would take out their men and take Peter? Who even knew he was back in the states? Paul wanted answers and could barely keep his composure. "Someone has to die for this" he said, standing up as he began to pace the room.

As he walked he noticed a small object come rolling up towards the feet of Watson. It was a green object and before he had completely figured out it was a problem... BOOOOOOOMMMMMMMM!!!! Instantly the body of C.W. Watson was mangled and his arms and legs were flying in the air and had landed at ease in several locations around the room. Brain matter wasn't too far behind and human flesh was the new decoration of the living room.

Paul Warner managed to crawl under a table and had survived the blast, but he was badly injured. His body was burnt and blood was leaking out of his ears. His arm appeared to be on the verge of being severed, due to a large piece of metal from the table that had positioned itself between his shoulder blade and the socket holding his left arm together.

Seconds later Paul heard another loud explosion that came from the back of the home. C.W. Watson's wife of thirty-five years died immediately.

147

She was unshielded and her body stood no chance against the vicious blast. He could smell the smoke and saw fires coming at him from all angles, so he knew he had to try and escape.

With each move he made the pain in his arm was so intense it halted him in his tracks. He was now choking off of the dark black smoke and trying his best not to ingest it, as well as get out of the house. Paul had to use what strength he had to hold the metal and his arm together, if he wanted to make it out the house alive.

Paul couldn't stand upright and hold his arm. His legs were wounded and bleeding and he could only crawl. He made his way past the head of his friend C.W. Watson and managed to make his way out into the backyard. He didn't know where he got the strength from because the pain itself was incredible. He just knew he didn't want to die inside of the house, which was quickly turning into a blazing inferno.

For the moment he felt safe as he lay on the grass in agonizing pain. He hadn't heard any noises besides the crackling from the flames and falling debris. Paul looked around and tried to see if he could see anyone. He needed help but all of Watson's neighbors lived a distance away, so he knew he'd have to get in his car and drive for help.

Paul forced himself to stand up and when he did, he noticed that something had fallen on to the ground. His arm, which was barely hanging on, was sawed off by all the moving he had done. The sharp metal had disconnected his arm, and although he was in shock he went into survival mode. He quickly took a piece of his shirt and stuffed it as deep as he could into the open wound. He limped to his car, which was in the front driveway, and with one arm he drove away from the burning home; while Watson and his wife's bodies burnt to a crisp.

Peter J. Greenberg had heard the loud explosions and he knew nothing but death had been perpetrated in the home. He could see the flames beginning to ignite and feared he was going to be tossed into the home so his body could be destroyed and any remnants of him would be untraceable.

When the three men had gotten back into the van, Peter was sitting still with his eyes closed. He didn't know what to do or say, so he just kept still. Fear penetrated the deepest cells in his body as he prayed for help, and in that moment the van was started and began moving again. Peter felt relieved and knew things would get better. He felt money could get him out of this because he hadn't been killed...but he had no clue he was headed back to Philadelphia.

Chapter 32
Hahnemann University Hospital...

Truck sat inside his car staring out of his window. He thought about walking into the hospital and approaching Face, man to man. Earlier he had seen Face for the first time rushing out of the hospital's front entrance and jumping into a waiting black Mercedes Benz. He watched as the car sped off in the opposite directions and was there when the car arrived later to drop Face off.

He kept telling himself that the right time was now and the more he tried to get out of the car, his fear kept him planted in the driver's seat. There were so many thoughts racing through his head and he didn't know which ones seemed logical or farfetched. All he knew for sure is that he wanted to talk to Face, and he'd have to get his courage up and make it happen or just leave.

Paul Warner drove himself to the nearest hospital, which was several miles away, and parked his car out front. His blood covered clothes had gotten the attention of staff, and as soon as he walked in through the doors he fell to the cold, hard ground.

Two male nurses rushed to his aid and one made the gruesome discovery that his left arm was missing. Paul was starting to lose consciousness because he had lost so much blood, and his life was heading south fast. An orderly had rushed over to the nurses and provided them with a gurney. As they lifted him they tried to keep him alert by asking his name and what had happened to him, but he wasn't responding. He couldn't speak but his eyes were open and he was thinking about who had kidnapped Peter, who had killed Watson and who had tried to kill him. A picture of Face emerged and then he shut his eyes and everything went black.

Later That Night
Bala Cynwyd, PA...

Veronica sat on the couch beating herself up about the terrible mistake she had made. Even though she knew Face would clean up her mess and take care of things, she knew she had been careless and put her friends' lives in danger. She had run her mouth, which was not only a stupid mistake but one for armatures. Veronica was a professional and thought she had hardened herself against being vulnerable; but she was wrong. She began to rethink her entire position in her business, as well as thinking about a possible early retirement.

Looming in her thoughts were the thoughts of Pamela. She had always been there for Veronica and Veronica knew she'd never forgive herself if she let anyone get to Face or Pamela. She sat in complete darkness and sipped on a glass of wine, hoping she would calm her nerves. She was scattered because she had just murdered a man, possibly ended her career, and her best friend was still in a coma.

West Philadelphia...

Peter J. Greenberg was inside of Doc's basement and he was tied down to a metal chair. Doc sat in the chair directly in front of him as he lustfully stared into his piercing ocean blue eyes. Peter had no clue who the man sitting opposite of him was, or why he had been sent to this location. No one had said a word to him yet, not even who was responsible for his kidnapping. He had thought the Russians were a possibility because they were known to be fearless and resourceful, but nothing had been confirmed.

Sounds of approaching footsteps had grabbed Peter's attention and he began to look around for the face that would match the feet. Once the body came into view, he saw a man dressed in army fatigues who was holding a gun.

Quincy removed the clothing-exposing his identity- and underneath he was wearing a black sweat suit. He was ready to kill Peter, just to off him and be done with him. Peter could sense this and once he saw the anger in Quincy eyes he did his best to look away or hold his head down. Then the stairs again began to talk, and the footsteps that led down the basement were the last pair he was thinking off.

Seeing Face was enough to make him faint. He couldn't believe it and now it all made sense. The Russians had nothing to do with his capture or the killings at Watson's home. The face of Norman "Face" Smith Jr. had made Peter J. Greenberg's greatest nightmare come to life. Face walked over to Peter's trembling body and shook his head in disgust;

and Reese who had just come in the basement shared his sentiment.

The basement was now filled with the player and the players, and Face reached over and snatched the duct-tape off of Peter's mouth.

"Face, please, please don't kill me."

"Why Peter…why would you ever cross me?"

"Please Face I beg you, just spare my life and I'll give you the money back. I'll give you more; I'll give you a billion dollars."

"Shut the fuck up you coward" Reese said, smacking the spit out of Peter's mouth.

Face placed his hand on Reese's shoulder, instructing him to calm down. He knew Reese or Quincy would take him out without a thought, but he needed things to be calm right now. Doc who sat there was so affixed to Peter's eyeballs that nothing being said or done could remove him from gazing upon them. It was surely creepy for Peter to have Doc staring so intensely in his face but he was a dead man pleading for his life, so he couldn't focus his full attention on Doc.

"A billion dollars" Face said, looking at Peter to see how serious he was about the offer. "Yes, a billion dollars with no strings attached and no bullshit. Just please don't kill me." Peter wasn't sure if he had made his case so he continued "If you have a computer we can get this done right now. The money will be wired from my account to yours in twenty minutes or less…I promise." Face looked at Quincy and said "Go get the laptop from out of the car." Quincy walked up the stairs to quickly retrieve the computer.

Face was starting to like this arrangement. He could get his money back and then a bonus. "Peter if you're lying to me I will kill you with my bare hands. Your eyeballs will pop out of your eyes sockets and I'll choke the life out of you." Peter was begging for Face to believe him. He wasn't about to tell anymore lies and especially when he knew Face had no other reason to keep him alive. "I'm telling you the truth. Just bring me a computer."

Moments later Quincy returned with the laptop. He passed the computer to Face and before handing Peter the laptop, Reese untied him. "Face, I know this might be going too far but please ask this guy to stop staring at me...this shit is freaking me out." Doc licked his lips and grinned. "No, he's fine. He may be many things but one of the best qualities that he has is his loyalty. Just focus on what we have going on." Doc was so happy to have Face take up for him and he looked at Peter and said "Your eyes are so beautiful."

Peter cut on the computer and did his best to ignore Doc's imminent gazes. He logged onto his personal offshore account and asked Face for some information so he could log into his bank. Face examined the computer to make sure Peter wasn't up to his old tricks. He had gotten Face out of millions before and it wasn't about to happen again.

Face still had his offshore accounts in the Cayman Island at the Atlantic International bank of Belize. He had changed all his passwords since Peter stole from him and now only Tasha and he had the current password. He knew he'd have to change the passwords immediately once Peter made the deposit into his account.

Doc was impressed to see that Peter had over five billion dollars in his account. His eyes lit up and he had never seen that much money in his life. He was stunned to know that the man with the beautiful blue eyes was also a man of great wealth. Doc wondered what he would do with that money if he had just a billion of it.

"I want it all." Peter was stunned. What was he saying? Did Face expect him to give him all the money he had to his name? "Every single penny of it will be mine or you just wrote out the date on your tombstone." Peter was sick. He loved his money and he was willing to share the billion but just couldn't understand giving it all away. How would he live, what would he do with himself? He couldn't think straight and was not in his right mind when he pleaded with Face. "Please…take a billion and let me walk out of here."

Face looked over at Quincy and nodded his head. Within a second Quincy was standing over Peter with his 9mm pointed directly at his forehead. "You have one minute to transfer it all…58, 57, 56." Face continued counting and when he got to 46, Peter said "Face, just promise me you won't kill me please" and then he began to finalize the transaction.

Doc walked over to Face and asked if he had a minute. It was obvious that business was being handled, but Doc had some things in mind he needed to discuss. "Doc, this isn't the best time" Face said, looking at Doc who was acting like someone who had a secret that they just couldn't hold any longer. "I

155

know but I have to speak to you now" Doc
demanded.

Face walked a few feet away and Doc
whispered in his ear. Face smiled at the information
he had just received and then patted Doc on the
shoulder, as he continued. "Doc, you're sure about
this" Face asked. "I'm a hundred percent positive.
I've been studying and researching how the Chinese
have done it for the last two years." Face smile and
said, "Okay Doc, he's all yours", and then he walked
back over to Peter.

"It's all done...you can check your account
now. All the money is there." Face took the laptop
computer and logged into his account. The money
was in his account and he now changed his
passwords before shutting down the computer. He
had his wealth back and then some; and was going to
make sure his team shared in the success. He didn't
show too much emotion because he was still in
constant worry of his mother but the slight grin was
enough to see that he was pleased to be sitting on
billions.

"Face, I've done it so can I please go now."
Face looked at Peter J. Greenberg and said "I'm not
going to kill you Peter. I gave you my word and
that's all a man has. None of my friends are going to
kill you either." Reese and Quincy were surprised to
hear his words. Why couldn't they get to him...he
was a snake and they would have gladly ended his
life. "Thank you Face, thank you. I'm so sorry about
everything. I really fucked up and I hope this clears
up any misunderstandings we had."

Just then Doc reappeared. No one even noticed that he walked away but now he was holding a long syringe in his hand. "I'm going to leave you in good hands with my friend here, he's a doctor. He's going to take good care of you because I know only a sick person would have stolen from me." Peter turned white. Any color this white man had inside of him had jumped out of his skin. He was panicking and didn't know what Doc had in store for him.

"Face you said your friends wouldn't kill me...you gave me your word." Face looked at Peter and said, "He's not going to kill you. He gave me his word." Peter just couldn't let his life end like this, he was desperate and he shouted out "Face, they want to kill you."

Face heard the intensity in his voice and said, "Who are they?"

"I don't know his name but he was working with Watson. They call him Paul. All he does is kill people."

"Peter, you'd say anything right now to get away from Doc."

"Yes I would but it doesn't make the facts any less true. He's coming after you."

Face took a moment and thought about the reports Mike had sent him. There was always another man with Watson but Mike had no real information on him. He had a physical description but no identifiable facts.

"What does he look like" Face asked, appearing to be quite interested in these new details. "He's short stocky and a bald headed man."

Face knew the description was correct from the photos he had gotten from Mike. Face looked at Peter J. Greenberg and said, "I'll take care of him just like I took care of his friend. Doc he's all yours."

Peter screamed like a baby; begging and pleading with Face to let him go. Reese, Quincy, and Face walked up the stairs and closed the door behind them. Doc was alone with his new toy and rushed towards Peter and injected the fluids of the syringe into his neck. The dosage was powerful and moments later Peter's body gave up all fight and though his eyes struggled to stay alert, they lost the battle and everything in the room went black.

Chapter 33
One Week Later...

Paul Warner had to be one of the luckiest men alive. To have survived a hand grenade explosion, with minimum damage to his hearing, a few burns on his legs and face, and the biggest lost being his left arm; he still felt he was a winner. Watson and his wife had no chance. What the grenade didn't take from them, the fire surely got. They both were pronounced dead at the scene, once the firefighters put the fire out and found their charred bones.

A special government task-force had been assembled to find out who put a hit out on the Senator. The only clues that they had were a few footprints they found near the Senator's home. They questioned Paul but he wasn't much help because he had plans of his own.

Once Paul left the hospital he compiled a list of names of people who would have wanted the Senator dead. He had a feeling in his gut it was a big-time drug lord because Watson was fighting the war on drugs. He was the head of the Anti-Drug Commission and in that business every drug lord and kingpin was his enemy. Three names immediately were placed at the list; Roberto Fuentes –who was the leader of the Los Rastrojos Cartel in Columbia, Semion Mogilevich-the wicked Ukrainian Crime Boss and leader of the Russian Mob, and Norman "Face" Smith Jr. also known to him as Black Scarface-who held the key to the United States drug empire.

Paul decided it would be his personal campaign to end the life of all three suspects. He always liked death in threes anyway. Justice had to be served and even though Watson wasn't there, he'd hold the torch for his old pal, and the committee that they both represented.

Inside of his Virginia home he sat at the edge of the bed thinking. He was wondering about the attack on the Senator's home, and all the moments that led up to the explosion; as well as the murders of the men guarding Peter J. Greenberg and his kidnapping. Then he thought about Agent Larry Sickler. He wondered where he was and why he still hadn't heard from him. Then as if it was an epiphany, he knew that all these occurrences could be tied back to one man-Face.

He was sure for moments but then questioned Face's power and ability. How did he have all this intelligence and he just didn't think Face would have the balls to come after them? One thing he was sure of was that Face would pay. If Face wanted a war Paul decided he was the man to give it to him; even if it was a silent one. He'd meet Face by using his sharpshooter skills. They didn't call him The Eraser for nothing and Paul was set on having his revenge.

He reached to pick up a copy of an old Washington Post newspaper he had on his bed. It was about a week old and when he read the headline '*U.S. Senator and Wife Murdered*' he began to become angry. He looked at his missing arm and said "Everyone must die."

Robbie had been a nervous wreck all week long. Whenever he went outside he kept his loaded .40 cal close by and often he'd drive with it on his lap; incase he needed to use it immediately. He was sure that people were following him around. Every time he saw someone he didn't recognize or a car he hadn't seen before, he'd panic. He was extremely paranoid and suffering from depression. Robbie was now using Arianna's pills daily.

Robbie was driving down 40th and Chestnut Street, when he noticed a tinted black van in his rear mirror. He quickly pulled over and grabbed his gun. He watched to see what move the van would make, but it just rode past him and turned at the end of the block.

His heart rate had shot up and his fingers were shaking. He couldn't start driving right away, so he reached in his glove compartment and pulled out his blunt. The blunt helped calm him and even if it was only temporary it was what worked. Since shooting his mother he had lost twenty pounds. Arianna was very worried for him and tried to make sure he ate but Robbie had no appetite. His stress was not just affecting his weight but his sleeping patterns were off. At night, Arianna would have to sleep with him for him to fall asleep; and then he'd only get an hour or so. Robbie would always be awaken from his sleep by nightmares, or from the fear that someone was about to kill him. Paranoia was now consuming his life.

Hahnemann University Hospital...

Face was standing outside of the hospital talking to Reese. People were coming and going. The hospital was located in the heart of downtown Philly; where traffic was often a constant and pedestrians filled the sidewalks. As the two discussed some important business and were getting a little fresh air, a familiar face approached them.

"Hey Face" Truck said. Face and Reese looked at each other confused but ready to make a move. They knew it was Truck, even though he had packed on a few more pounds. They couldn't believe this rat-bastard had the balls to show his face in Philly; and further for him to come up to the hospital-he was out of order. "Face, man please can I talk with you?"

Reese was ready to take care of Truck right away. He had no business showing his face to either one of them and what could he have to say. "What the fuck you want to talk about nigga" Reese said. "Be cool Reese, not here anyway" Face said, trying to calm down the mood and find out what Truck was doing there. "I don't want no trouble, I just want to talk" Truck said, in a timid weak voice. "Nigga you testified against me. You've said plenty" Face said, trying to control the anger he truly felt. "I'm gonna kill your rat ass. We can talk at your funeral" Reese said.

Face understood the anger, Truck had testified against them but he asked Reese to calm down once more. They were at a very public place and Face didn't' want any commotion to jump off with his

162

mother upstairs. Face looked at Truck and said "Let's go have a seat over by that bench." Reese didn't want to do anything but kill Truck, but he gave the area a look over to see if they were being set up by Truck, and then stood guard as Face and Truck walked towards the bench and sat down.

"I never wanted to rat you out. I swear I didn't. I felt like I had no way out and I was facing so much time. The Feds cut me a deal and I just didn't see how I could ever get out of prison if I didn't take the deal. It wasn't what I wanted, they just jammed me up."

"So you went against the code for your freedom?"

Truck put his head down, knowing he had made a mistake. Before he could answer the question, Face excused himself and got up from the bench. He had just gotten a phone call to his cellphone. After a short conversation he returned to the bench and took his seat.

"I can never forgive you if that's why you came here. What you did was dishonorable and no one should rat. I don't care if you were looking at life but you wasn't. You was in the game and when you in the game sometimes doing time comes with the territory."

"Face, I know you can't understand but I'm sorry man."

"Wasn't you in the witness protection program" Reese asked, now trying to see what was really Truck's reason for showing up.

"Yeah, but I left the program. I need to make this situation here right."

"I was your friend, and you were the snitch. It can't

163

ever be right. You gotta go Truck, your time is up."

Reese was glad that Face was sending Truck away. There was nothing for them to discuss because Truck would never be respected or trusted again. Truck was still hopeful that maybe Face would reconsider. "Face please man. I'm really fucked up...I ain't got shit. I'm homeless...man I'm fucked up." Reese knew all bets were off and said "Nigga, didn't he tell you to roll. What you fuckin hard of hearin, kick rocks you snitch."

They watched as Truck got up from the bench and made his way across the street. As soon as he got into the car a tall black man approached the driver's side window and with his loaded 9mm-silencer attached- and when he pulled the trigger he shattered the window, and filled Truck's head up with hot lead.

He had no chances and not even a moment to scream for help. In the crowded area no one had realized what had truly happened and by the time the assailant had gotten in his car and drove away, the job was done and none were the wiser.

Quincy had called Face while he was sitting on the bench, and Face gave word for Quincy to send Kyle to take care of Truck. The idea that Truck thought he would come up to the hospital and beg for forgiveness was unforgivable. As Reese and Face watched Truck cross the street, they had already crossed him off their list of enemies; which was quickly becoming much shorter.

Chapter 34
Broad Street & Erie Avenue...

Robbie pulled up and parked his car in front of Black and Nobel Bookstore. This was his father's old stomping ground and he was less cautious about anything happening to him here. He saw a group of men who were held up in conversations and yelled to them "Yo, Big Phil and Tyson y'all got a minute."

Tyson and Big Phil saw who it was and Tyson said "Yo, give us a quick minute." The two put their conversations on hold and walked over to Robbie. "What's up Hood Jr." Big Phil asked, shaking his hand and giving him a hug. "What's the word on the street...I'm hearing a lot of shit on my name and I just ain't feelin it" Robbie said, looking at Tyson.

Tyson was a straight shooter. He wasn't about to mince words when the youngster needed to hear the truth. "Shit ain't good right now. Word done got to me that you're the man who shot Face's mom. That's what the word is." Big Phil knew it was better for him to get it straight too, so he didn't interfere when Tyson gave it to Robbie direct. "I heard it in the barbershop and it done made its rounds all over" Big Phil said, as the two started to walk away from Robbie. Rumor or truth, the two knew they wanted no parts of the penalties that Robbie was facing.

Unfortunately, Robbie was nothing but trouble and a standing target as well. Just like his father, who had been in loads of trouble twenty years ago, Robbie had now followed in his footsteps. Tyson didn't want to see any harm come to Robbie, so he said to him

"Take care of yourself and your beautiful sister…but always watch yourself out here."

As Robbie made his way to his car Big Phil and Tyson watched him nervously get into the vehicle. They had been around long enough to know that Robbie was just checking to see if the word was true. He knew how the streets were and he was coming to get some type of validation that the word was out. When he pulled off Big Phil looked at Tyson and said "Damn shame, he's a dead man walking."

Near Broad & Snyder
South Philadelphia…

"Not bad" Ron Perry said, as he looked at himself in the mirror. He was dressed in a black tailor-made suit, and he was getting ready to celebrate his 25th Anniversary at the North American Motor Inn on City Line Avenue. As he finished looking at himself he thought about taking his gun. He felt naked without it but he had promised his wife he was going to come without it. She didn't want this night to be about work, she just wanted the two of them to enjoy themselves; and he wanted the same.

After grabbing his car keys the thought of bringing his gun had come back into his head. Many police officers and detectives would never leave home without their piece. It was a tough decision and after giving it a few more minutes he decided to make his lady happy, he had to leave it.

Ron Perry went through the ritual of checking all the windows and the back door, before setting the alarm and walking out of the house. He got in his car and looked into the mirror and said "I've waited twenty five years for this day and tonight I'm going to enjoy this one." He started up his car and excitingly headed towards the North American Motor Inn.

Hahnemann University Hospital...

Face stood over his mother's bed praying. He was in deep prayer because he was filled with such agony and pain. He needed his mother. He had never felt such pain in his life...he was truly missing his mother's spirit and wanted to see her happy and smiling once more. Face wasn't sure of his mother's future but didn't want this to be the depths of his mother's life; so he prayed and prayed and tried to believe that a change was coming real soon.

When Face lifted his head up Reese was standing by the door. Face bent down and gave his mother a kiss on her forehead and walked out of the room with Reese.

"What's up? You ready for tonight" Face asked.

"Yeah, I'm ready. Actually I can't wait. How you holding up."

"I'm doing my best...I'd be doing so much better if she'd just same something."

"I know man...how's Tasha and the kids."

"They're alright. They keep asking about their grandma and I can't tell them nothing. I don't know how she's doing."

"You've got a lot on your plate man but keep praying. I'm praying too."

"You know I'm going to do that. Did you check up

on Veronica?"

"Sure did. She's still a little shaken up but doing a lot better than she was. She'll be alight."

"Reese, I'm a need you to keep your cool man. Sometimes I can see you ready to pop off but things have changed. We running shit and gotta do shit smoothly. I know you can handle all the things we got coming down the pipe but I want to make sure we're cool with that temper…"

"Enough said. It's under control. We've come too far and I'm not going back or fucking up what we got going."

"Good, where's Quincy?"

"We meeting up later but he's on that other task we talked about."

"Cool, how's that coming?"

"Oh, we ready when you're ready."

"Crazy thing is it's killing me but I gotta do this. He violated and he's going to pay for this."

"Then what are you waiting for?"

"It's hard. I feel ready but then…it's crazy."

Reese saw what a conflicting decision his friend had to make; but he knew he had to make it. Reese had seen him go through rough patches before but this was different. With Pamela in a coma Reese knew not much in life mattered to him anymore. Face eyes were heavy and the inner turmoil was taking a toll on him. Reese gave him a hug before existing and said "When you're ready, we ready. Just call me if you need anything."

Face walked back to his mother's room. He hadn't been the same men since leaving the Bahamas and he wasn't sure if he'd ever be the same. He had to deal with his enemies who not only wanted him dead but his family too. Robbie, his own brother had done the unthinkable and left Face with a great dilemma. He had truly loved his brother and no one could have told him he'd be his greatest enemy. Robbie had taken the position that was once held by his father Hood; and Face knew there was only one outcome for a man who stood in that spot-DEATH BY ANY MEANS NECESSARY!

Washington, D.C...

Inside the Arlington National Cemetery a private burial was being held for U.S. Senator C.W. Watson. In attendance were some of the most powerful men and women in U.S. politics. The President and Vice President were there, along with the Secretary of State, The Attorney General, The House Speaker, and many Senators and Congressman had come to pay their final respects. For over thirty years, Watson had been one of the most powerful men in the states. He had made many friends and just as many enemies.

As the catholic priest stood over his navy casket, he gave a touching final prayer. Just a few feet away Paul Warner stood in the back, angry and relieved at the same time. He knew that he could have been lying inside of the casket, and he also knew who was responsible for placing his good friend in his final resting place.

Seeing Paul visible upset, the Vice President approached him.

"Are you okay Paul?"

"No Mr. Vice President I am not. This is not
acceptable."

"Then you know what you must do. You have my
full support and assistance. If you need me I'm just
a phone call away."

"Thank you Sir, I appreciate that."

Paul watched as the Vice President turned and
walked away. His words were comforting but didn't
heal the emotional wounds Paul was feeling. Paul
was known as a tough guy but today his emotions
had gotten the best of him. Before today he could
adorn his poker face at any event but he couldn't
control himself now. He had sent several men,
women, and children to their graves and it never
bothered him. Brining death to people was a job,
nothing more and a job he loved. He was a man that
many people feared and a man that would hold a
grudge until he settled the score.

Paul knew he had to make things right
because he needed to have control over his emotions.
He could not allow Face to get the best of him, he
just couldn't.

**Near 12th & Vine Street
Center City...**

When Robbie walked into his condo he didn't
pay attention to the tall black man who was standing
across the street. He had been watching Robbie and
Arianna for weeks, and was learning their every
move; from the time they left the house and how
long, where they went, who they spoke to, what car

they drove, and any intimate details he could get on the two.

It didn't take much to learn about the two, they were wide open. They had not learned to be cautious and Robbie with his paranoia had become quite sloppy and foolish. He was trying to live off his father's reputation but he didn't have the heart or skills to do him any justice.

For now Quincy had all he needed, and he knew that Robbie would soon be dealt with…very soon.

Chapter 35
Ibiza Valencia, Spain...

Roberto Fuentes had just received word that a special U.S. taskforce had been assembled to capture him and bring him to America so he could be tried. The messenger stated he was the prime suspect in the murder of Senator C.W. Watson. This was funny to Roberto who knew that Watson had many enemies and that anyone in the drug business could have wanted him killed.

Standing on the deck of his 40 foot Yacht, he stood carefree smoking on his Cuban cigar. As he blew the thick greyish smoke into the air, he was suddenly approached from behind. The long pair of arms wrapped around him belonged to beautiful Latin woman. She softly kissed his neck and when he turned around she was standing nude; and her body was being kissed by the sun.

This woman was beautiful and there was not a flaw to be seen. She had a beautiful face, perfect breast, perfect lips, long sexy legs, curves in all the right places and an ass that would put most to shame.

Roberto took no time removing his shorts and top. He had no real concerns about what was going on in the states but it was his job to keep abreast of any happenings that could possible interfere with his lifestyle. He lay back in the lounge chair as the beauty mounted him, and the two made passionate love for all to see.

For days Doc had been on the Internet ordering all the items he needed to complete his experiment. He was a man on a mission and nothing was going to stand in the way of his newest desire to do the impossible. He had contacted companies in India and those in Southern France to get what he needed. Everything had to be perfect so he wasn't concerned with the price or where it came from.

There was an abundance of thoughts racing in Doc's head, and he had to take an eyeball break so he could calm down and regroup. Human parts were becoming his next obsession because he had eaten the toes, fingers, and ears from the crossing guard's body. But now he had a new project and he was willing to do what he had to so it would go off without a hitch. Plus he had given his friend his word that he'd be able to complete his project successfully; and he wasn't going to disappoint him.

The sound of the doorbell startled Doc and took his attention away from his Internet search. Doc looked at the surveillance camera to see who had disturbed his important work. He was happy to see that the UPS man had two large boxes for him. He loved getting packages, especially when he needed the objects to complete his projects. "Yes, it's finally here" Doc said, as he rushed up the stairs and out of the basement.

Belmont & City Line Avenue...

The North American Motor Inn was crowded with people, including several Philadelphia Police Officers. Inside of the ballroom people were dancing, eating, talking and enjoying themselves. The food was a big hit and Ron's wife sister had used her catering services to supply and serve the delicious food. Detective Ron Perry was surrounded by a group of his colleagues and he was having a great time. They were making jokes and laughing at everything, because by now the liquor had been piled on heavy.

Once a co-worker called out for a toast, everybody returned to their seats for the champagne toast. Ron and his wife were seated at a table with the Mayor, The Chief of Police, and a few members of City Council. The toast was very kind and Ron's wife was so impressed by the touching words his co-workers had started to share for the lovely couple. Many people joined in with one-liners and some had plenty to say about the couple. Twenty-five years of marriage was nothing to sneeze at and those who knew Ron knew how much he loved his wife.

Ron had felt the urge to get to the lavatory so he excused himself and made his way to the restroom. Once in the bathroom he found a private stall and went inside to handle his business. He hadn't been paying attention to the set of eyes that had been on him all night, nor did he feel cautious when he heard someone enter the restroom.

There were five private stalls separating the two men from each other. In one stall, the man who had just made his way in the bathroom was removing his catering uniform and placing his silencer onto his weapon, while the other was emptying his belly.

There was a knock on the stall that Ron Perry was in. He was in deep concentration. He said "I'll be out in a minute" not noticing that there were other vacant stalls. Then without notice the door had been kicked open while Ron was seated on the toilet. "What the fuck" Ron said, trying to use his hands to cover himself. Reese removed his fake mustache and his catering hat and looked at Ron Perry and said "Pay backs a bitch, ain't they." Before entering the restroom Reese made sure two of his men were on the door, so no one else entered the bathroom.

Ron Perry couldn't speak because he knew exactly who Reese was. He knew what he had taken from him but he never expected to be caught in this situation. "Remember me mother fucker? This is for Momma and my little brother." Reese ferociously pulled the trigger and let his 9mm blow holes in Ron's head and chest.

Ron Perry's body lay flopped on the toilet and Reese looked at him and said "I got him for you mom and you too baby brother. Y'all rest easy now." Quincy came into the bathroom to check on Reese and took the clothes Reese had and placed them in large back pack. Then he handed him a change of clothing, which was a valet parking uniform and the two left out of the side entrance, but not before they locked the bathroom and put an out-of-order sign on the door.

Chapter 36
Four Days Later...

Inside of the F.B.I. offices in downtown Philadelphia, a group of top agents sat around a large round table. F.B.I. director James Conner was heated and after weeks of investigations, with no evidence linking a suspect to the murders of his two agents or their wives, he started to feel they weren't doing all they could to close these cases. The needed someone arrested and would do anything they could to get this killer off the street.

James Conner would not rest until he got a conviction. He had come up the ranks with Agents McDonald and Powaski and they were good friends of his. He knew he had what it took to solve the crimes because he was known for solving unsolvable crimes. He had a suspect list, but he had to make the motive tie into the crime, along with the evidence, if he had any chance of making a conviction stick in a court of law. Norman "Face" Smith Jr. was his suspect. He was the only man who made sense in this case but Conner needed proof.

They were also looking into the deaths of C.W. Watson, the guards who had been guarding Peter, Ron Perry, Vernon "Truck" Wilson, and the suspicious disappearance of Peter J. Greenberg. Paul Warner had called James Conner and suggested that Face was behind it all. He told him he couldn't prove it but he was certain he was the mastermind behind the crime. He also told him that Face was much more powerful than they had ever thought and they needed to watch him closer than ever before.

James Conner respected the tip but had to
work off proof. If they didn't have anything to tie
Face to the crimes it was not going to solve his cases.
He was aware of Face's last run in with the U.S.
Government and how they had taken a beaten; he was
not about to make a fool out of the Administration
again. However, he realized that the more Paul talked
to him on the phone he wasn't concerned about
taking Face to court. Paul was talking about the
elimination of Face and his entire family. This was
something James Conner wasn't trying to play into;
especially over the phone.

Bellagio Hotel & Casino
Atlantic City, New Jersey...

Karen Brown was living in a world of bliss
and ecstasy. Inside of a large walk-in shower Quincy
was fucking her hard from behind. As the warm
water soothed her body and Quincy's dick mollified
her pussy, the moans of passion escaped into the
steamed filed air. Karen was on cloud nine and
enjoying each and every moment.

Quincy leaned forward and bit down hard on
the back of Karen's neck, and then he reached his
arms around and cupped her huge breast. "Whose
pussy is this" he demanded. She responded
enthusiastically and certain "Yours Daddy, it's all
yours Daddy!"

For the next hour Quincy fucked her
throughout their elegant hotel suite; giving her the
pleasure she was addicted to. Karen was a valuable
asset to Face and Quincy. She kept the guys two steps

ahead of the F.B.I. and as long as he kept the information coming, Quincy made it his business to give her the dick she craved. Karen was willing to do anything for Quincy and she had gotten so deeply involved she had long forgotten about any consequences. Karen's thoughts were consumed with Quincy and being fucked by him, twenty-four hours a day.

Inside the Laurel Hill Cemetery, hundreds of Philadelphia Police Officers watched as the golden casket of Detective Ron Perry was being readied to go into its final resting place. Four days earlier Ron Perry's body was found in the bathroom after a staff member of the North American Motor Inn was instructed to see why the restroom was locked. The staff member threw up at the site of the bloodied bullet-filled body and screamed for help. The murder was a great source of embarrassment for the police and detective divisions, because many of them were on-site but no one knew what had happened.

Robbie and Arianna stood a few feet away from the casket and were overwhelmed with emotion. Uncle Ron had always protected them and looked after them. He was very close to them and they had little to no family already. When Robbie heard what had happened it only put more stress in his life and made him wonder if he was next. Everyone he had loved ended up dead and now he was feeling so vulnerable.

Flowers were now being laid onto the casket and Arianna grabbed her brother's hand as they walked to the casket and placed their red roses on top. Before walking to their limousine they stopped to embrace Ron's wife. She was barely able to stand and had to be assisted by her sister and brother to keep upright. She had lost her voice and was in such a state of shock that once they hugged her, they quickly rushed off to their limo.

Once Robbie and Arianna were in the car, they broke down in each other's arms. This was a day of sorrow and so much pain and misery surrounded their lives. The two siblings were stressed, worn, and truly tired out.

Chapter 37

Face was seated in the passenger seat of his Mercedes Benz, while Reese drove the car. They were headed to Chester, PA, to meet up with Quincy and a few of their men at a private location. Now with the heat turned up all cars were checked for tracking devices and everyone was alert to see if they were being followed.

Face knew the Government was not about to leave him alone and that they had never gotten over him because he had beaten them at their own game. He knew those tapes were even more valuable now and though they had a feeling that he was responsible and connected to the recent murders; they would not come out swinging unless they were willing to incriminate judges, lawyers, senators and many other high profile political figures. Their careers would be destroyed and the risk was something many were not willing to take; especially if they didn't have the evidence to put Face away for the rest of his life; or to get him the death penalty.

As the ride continued, Face thought of his mother as his cellphone began to vibrate inside of his pockets. The only problem was that it wasn't his phone; it was Agent's Larry Sicklers phone. "Hello" Face said. "Larry is that you" a man said, sounding concerned. Face didn't say a word. "Larry is everything okay, it's Paul and I've been worried sick." Face kept quiet and listened to see if Paul would say more but he didn't. Face ended the call.

Moments later the phone began to vibrate again but Face didn't answer this time. Face knew that he had just heard the voice of his newest enemy, the man that Peter warned him about. The man that wanted him dead…but Face was already two steps ahead of him.

Hahnemann University Hospital…

Veronica and Tasha were talking and sat a few feet away from Pam's hospital bed. They had just finished praying for her and they also talked to her, so she could hear their voices. Tasha was telling Veronica about how the kids were begging her to teach them how to drive. They had sworn up and down that they knew how to and that they were old enough, and the story had the girls caught up in laughter.

Once the laughter had subsided Veronica heard a soft moan and she looked at Tasha and they rushed over to Pam's bed. "Ahhh", they didn't understand what she was saying and they couldn't care, they were just so happy to see she was saying something. "Pam can you hear me, its V my love. I love you, can you say something." Pam tried to make out a word but it was low and they didn't get it. "Oh lord my baby is alive, and she's going to be alright Tasha, run get the doctor" Veronica said, as the ladies were jumping around and filled with enthusiasm.

Tasha ran to the nurses' station in tears and told the nurse to come in to Pam's room because she had woken up. While at the desk, Veronica was holding Pam's hand and telling her she loved her. She was crying and filled with joy. "Face…Face" Pam said, as she began to slowly open up her eyes.

"Baby, he's not here but he'll be here soon trust me. He's been here with you and he loves you so much. We all do." Pamela began to squeeze Veronica's hand and began to say "Face...Face."

Two doctors rushed into the room and started to check all of Pamela's vital signs and brain waves. They were so excited to see her awake and though it may have been personal for her visitors, doctors are often enthused by the medical side of a patient's recovery. They wanted to know what brought her out of the coma, if the ladies had seen her do anything before she woke up, or if they had said something different to her today.

As the doctors continued to do their medical evaluations, Pamela continued to call for her son Face. Tasha and Veronica were so excited that she was going to be okay and both women were in tears.

Chapter 38
Washington DC...

Inside of The Oval office of the United States, the President sat at his desk as the Vice President; Charles Bush, paced back and forth throughout the room. As the President read the confidential documents that were in front of him, he'd occasionally lift his head up and shake it in disgust. All the information he was now reading was new to him and he couldn't believe he had just gotten his hands on these documents.

Once he was done reading the documents, he removed his glasses and sat them on his desk. Then he stood up and walked over to his VP. "So Charles you're telling me that some street thug is responsible for the death of C.W. Watson and his wife?" Charles was sure of his source and said "Yes Mr. President, that's what my sources say." The President wasn't pleased with this and said "Your sources, who are your source?" Charles responded, "Sir, that information I can't divulge. I also don't want you to be privileged to sources that could come back to haunt your career."

The President shook his head in agreement. He was not about to put his political career in jeopardy. "I can't believe that this Black Scarface character has this much power. He was able to take out Watson and his wife in their home, but left behind no evidence. How does this happen Charles?" The VP didn't know what to say. "How did he know where Watson lived? How did he come up on that piece of information?" The VP wanted to provide concrete answers but all he could go on was speculations. "I've been considering as many possibilities as I could and I think this may have been an inside job. Agent's information and home addresses are confidential and not public knowledge, so I've been thinking we need to look within. Watson was well guarded and I'm not sure how anyone could have gotten that close to him."

The President knew Charles had brought this to his attention for a reason. No one goes through having confidential documents presented to the President just for viewing purposes. "So Charles, what do you want from me?" The VP was glad that he had asked because he needed the President to help him get Face. "Sir, I need your approval so we can set up a special taskforce to take him down." The President thought over what his VP had asked and quickly responded, "Charles I won't do it. I can't put money towards that based off of speculations and unfounded fact. If it ever got out to the public that I wasted money on a phantom, my political career would go down the garbage. I've fought hard to get where I am and being the first black President I will not allow any connections to a street thug to be the end of what I've built."

Charles pretended to understand The President's reasons as he made his way out of The Oval Office; but he had already spoken to Paul Warner and approved a budget that would allow him to get enough men to take Face out. This would be a secret that would have to stay between the VP and Paul Warner because he had gotten no support from the Commander in Chief.

The Vice President had his own agenda with Face. It had been a lot deeper than anyone could imagine. For twenty-five years Watson and the VP shared a secret. The two were undercover lovers and the love they shared for each other was profound. Many people in political office had been accused of being bi-sexual or homosexual, but Charles always knew an accusation was better than a proven fact. He wished he could come out and say his lover was killed by a drug dealer thug but his wife and family would lose their minds. He had to protect them and his political career.

When he got to his office he opened his desk and pulled out a small photo he kept hidden in his desk. It was his favorite photo of Watson when the two of them had traveled to the Virgin Islands. He stared at his photo and then said "I miss you my love" before kissing the picture and placing it back in his desk. Charles' heart was in pain and he mourned the loss of his homosexual lover, and didn't want his killer to walk away scot-free.

Later That Evening
Hahnemann University Hospital...

Inside of his mother's hospital room, Face stood there holding her hand. She had awakened from her coma but still wasn't fully aware of her surroundings or about what had happened to her. Every so often she would softly call out for Face or try to say hello, and then she would doze off.

Seeing his mom like this wasn't easy. He wanted her back to her old self and the doctor's

185

explained to him Pamela would need physical therapy and it could be intensive once they saw the full range of her current condition. They also told him that her memory wasn't fully intact and with time they would be able to tell him more.

"Face...Face" Pamela cried out. Her son wasn't going anywhere and he fought back his tears as he looked at his mom. She was a much smaller woman since being admitted to the hospital, and although she was being fed through a feeding tube, she still had lost too much weight. She wasn't sure of where she was and was not speaking clearly, but Pamela was a fighter and Face knew it. He had to stay strong because he wanted his strength to fuel hers.

As Face thought about the reason his mother was barely alert and unable to care for herself, his rage towards his brother grew. He no longer had compassion for him and now wished he had killed Robbie the night he had killed Hood. Not one of his enemies had burned him as deeply as Robbie had. He had fucked with his mother and Face was not about to let Robbie walk the streets anymore. Robbie had eliminated their bond when he shot his mother and now Face was going to finish the job he should have completed a long time ago.

Chapter 39
One Week Later
Downtown Philadelphia...

Inside of the crowded Reading Terminal Market, Veronica, Tasha, and Passion were shopping for fresh fruits and vegetables. The famous Reading Terminal Market was one of Philly's most popular establishments and was well known for the freshness and quality of their meats and produce. People from all ethnic backgrounds are frequent shoppers of the large food warehouse; where they can get a value for their bucks without losing out on the quality.

As the women walked around shopping, there was someone looming close by. The female prowler had noticed Tasha from some of her newspaper articles. She knew that the beautiful woman she was looking at was the successful wife of Norman "Face" Smith Jr.; the man who had killed her parents.

Arianna stayed as close as she could to the trio without being detected. Tasha had once been a woman that she admired. When she read about her accomplishments in the real-estate business and how she gave back to her community, she thought of her as a role model to young woman, but being Face's wife was something she could never respect. Face was Arianna's enemy and so was Tasha.

Reaching into her Gucci pocketbook, Arianna pulled out her 9mm and walked towards Tasha and her two friends. She was filled with nervousness but she wanted revenge. She knew that she hadn't been able to get close to Face and getting Tasha would be

187

good enough for her. She wanted Face to suffer and she knew this would hit home.

Arianna was in close range of Tasha but then two police officers appeared. It wasn't surprising that they would be in the Reading Terminal Market because there were often cops there; but it was just her luck they would appear just as she was ready to make her move. She quickly placed her gun back into her pocketbook and calmly walked away. She knew there would be another time and place, she was sure of it.

Once outside she walked to 9th and Market so she could catch the 23 Septa bus that would take her to Temple University. She was hoping to have good news to tell Robbie, who she was supposed to meet in an hour, but she remained hopeful because she was going to have her revenge.

Northeast Philly...

As Reese stood in front of Momma's tombstone, the white snowflakes softly fell down from the grey colored sky. Reese had awakened early that morning and dove to the cemetery alone. Momma's death had never stopped haunting him. Even with the frustration and stresses he faced when he was in prison, there was never a day that passed when he didn't think about Momma or DJ. He had fallen into a deep depression while incarcerated, and had sought the help of a psychiatrist to help him deal with their deaths. At times he thought talking about it helped, but their faces would visit him in his sleep and bring the pain back even stronger.

The snowflakes started to cover Momma's tombstone, so Reese got on his knees and wiped the snow away. He placed a dozen of red roses and white stargazer lilies on her grave, as he said a silent prayer. Then with his head bowed, he reached his arms up and let out a scream of rage. The wind carried his scream off into the air as it grew silent.

Reese kept his eyes closed and said "Momma I got him for you...I got him Momma." For the next few minutes he sat there and stared at the tombstone. He wished that he could turn back the hands of time and make things right. Momma died too early and DJ never even had a chance to live his life.

Once he stood up he still didn't feel better. He had gotten his revenge but what he wanted most was impossible. He made the short trek back to his car, leaving a trail of footprints that were filled with pain.

Inside of his Virginia home, Paul Warner walked out of the shower and into his bedroom. He began to dry himself off and then he stared at himself in front of the long oval mirror above his dresser. He looked at his wounds and more so at his left shoulder; where an arm used to be attached. The tragic event played in his head and then replayed over and over, and the frustration in him grew. He was now disabled and had to learn how to do everything-which once came with ease-with just one arm.

He knew most men would never be able to bounce back as he had. He wasn't going to sit around and beg for assistance. He was going to learn how to survive and make the best out of a horrible situation. He wasn't worried about money because he was a wealthy man; but fixing the man who took his mobility away from him was of great precedence. Face was his man and he knew it, and it was only a matter of time before he would have a chat with this Black Scarface.

Chapter 40
West Philadelphia...

Doc opened his front door and he was filled with excitement. He was like a child on show-and-tell day and he couldn't wait to have his friends see his new project. After weeks of operations and preparations, the moment had finally arrived where he could show off his finalized project.

Reese, Quincy, and Face followed Doc through the house, down into the well-lit basement. Once in the basement no one there could believe their eyes. They were dumbfounded and speechless. Doc took their silence as a sign of amazement and began jumping up and down. He was so proud of his creation and couldn't wait to speak.

"I told you I could do it, I told you Face. Look at her...you can't even tell." Face walked up to Peter J. Greenberg and he was amazed. He could see no traces of the man who was once his financial advisor. All Face could do was shake his head in disbelief because Doc had done the impossible. He had literally transformed Peter into a blonde woman; and she was beautiful.

Doc had surgically transformed Peter into a female. He had operated and removed his penis, and then went through the process of creating a vagina. Daily he would insert dildo's to keep the wound open, and he gradually increased the size to ensure the opening would be able to stay open and handle an average size penis during sex. Peter's face had been reconstructed to have a softer appeal and all facial hair, except for his eyebrows and eyelashes had been

191

removed. He had his chest reconstructed and given a firm pair of breast as well as a new ass.

"That's Peter" Reese asked. "Yes, Yes, Yes, but her name is now Marabella" Doc said. He walked over to his masterpiece and said "I took out her vocal cords so she can't talk and she's given lots of female hormones to keep a feminine appearance. She's so beautiful." Quincy was still in shock and didn't have any questions. He was always creped out by Doc and this had taken him to a new level of creepy and craziness.

Doc was still on a high and said "Look at her ass. That's the best ass money can buy. China sure knows how to make them." As the men looked at the surgically enhanced ass, they could not deny that it was a nice ass. Doc continued, "I had to give her a little something to put her out because I knew you guys were coming. She has some rough days and I thought seeing you guys might put some added stress on her, so today I let her get some extra rest."

Doc had a slave living in his basement. Marabella was locked up all day long and against her will had been turned into a woman. Face found it hard to look at his former financial advisor because he still couldn't believe that he had been turned into a female.

"Damn what you did Doc is worse than death. You turned this no good nigga into a good looking bitch" Reese said, as everyone erupted into laughter. Reese was curious about what Doc had done. He had never heard of anyone getting their dick cut off and being a woman so he had to ask. "Do you fuck her Doc?" Doc was more than eager to answer. "No not yet. Her vagina is not healed yet but as soon as it does we will make love."

Quincy burst into laughter because he was sure Doc was insane. Doc was talking about Peter like this was normal and he had found his perfect lover. Quincy started to look closer at Marabella's face and he noticed Doc had enhanced the lips and gave her a nose job. It was mind boggling and Quincy had had his fill. He was ready to go because in the back of his mind he could be next.

Reese complimented Doc on a job well done. He was impressed by the work, while Quincy was slightly disturbed by the passion Doc showed with this new project. As the two men made their way upstairs Face stayed behind to have a word with Doc. "Great work Doc. You did a really nice job."
"Thanks so much Face, I'm really proud of her."
"Listen, I'm going to need your services real soon."
"You know I'm here, just let me know when."
"I need a removal, just like you did before."
"Oh, yes…I remember and I loved doing it."
"Alright Doc, I will need you tomorrow night."
"Tomorrow will be perfect. I can't wait!"

Doc walked Face out and made his way back downstairs to Marabella. He couldn't wait to put her tits in his mouth and as he sucked them he dreamed of the moment when he could penetrate her. It was a desire that he had to try so hard to resist. He didn't want to infect her newly created vagina, so he forced himself to wait.

As the men got into their car they drove down the snowy streets, still in disbelieve. Face said

"Marabella" and they all laughed, as they drove to their next destination down on South Street.

Chapter 41
Early the Next Day...

Arianna and one of her friends from school decided to take a weekend trip to Atlantic City. She wanted to get way for a few days just to clear her mind but at first she thought it would be better if she stayed home with Robbie. He wanted his sister to get a break and told her it would be good for her to get away from all the drama they had recently gone through. She wanted Robbie to come but he didn't want to, besides he felt she'd be in better company with her girlfriend Jasmine.

After packing her bags, Robbie carried them outside to the car. Jasmine was in the driver's seat all ready to go and he didn't want to hold them up. "You ready to win some money and have a good time" he asked, as he kissed his sister and opened up the car door for her. He then placed her bags into the trunk of the car and went back to the passenger's side to give his sister one last kiss on the cheek.

"Okay, pull off and have fun" Robbie said. Arianna smile and Jasmine said "We will" and then she pulled off. Robbie watched the car pull down the block and then he went back inside their condominium.

"How is everything going my good friend?"
"Roberto, everything is going much better. I should be seeing you soon."
"I've heard some disturbing news recently."

"What's up?"

"Your Vice President and some other top U.S. politicians are trying to get me. They are all members of a secret organization called the C.O.U.P., and they got me at the top of their most wanted list...they are calling me a terrorist and say I'm a major threat to America."

"The C.O.U.P.? That's sounds like some illuminati shit but I didn't get that message."

"Yes, it's true so we have to be very cautious and they can't know that we have a relationship. They are a very powerful organization."

"No problem. just know that I'm here when you need to contact me."

"I know that, that's why I chose to work with you and to make you a part of my family."

"Why don't you get away for a while?"

"I did, I left Columbia for a while and came to Peru I took a little vacation."

"Enjoy yourself, and we'll talk soon."

When the conversation ended, Face was thankful that he had taken extra steps to rid himself of any possible trackers and glad that he invested in spy equipment. Doc had told him about a chip that could be inserted into his cellphones that made the signal untraceable, and they could not be bugged. Doc spent countless hours on the Internet and would always let Face know about the latest gadgets.

He wasn't surprised about the news he had gotten from Roberto because he knew how the government was. They watched anyone who was getting drugs into the country and would do what they could to get a piece of the pie.

Face walked back into his mother's room and went back to talking to her and holding her hand. He had a big day ahead of him and a pressing task to complete; Face could not wait.

That Evening
Villanova, PA...

Tasha, Veronica and Passion sat around the living room watching a re-run of '*The Real Housewives of Atlanta*'. Since Pamela was shot, the three of them had gotten a lot closer and they needed each other for moral support.

While they sat on the sofa sipping wine and laughing at Ne-Ne, Lil Norman walked over to his mother and asked to speak to her in his room. Tasha saw that her son was in a serious mood-and this was not his usual demeanor-so she quickly got up and followed him to his bedroom.

Once she was in the room she closed the door and they both sat on the end of the bed. Lil Norman looked up at her with his watery filled eyes and said "Momma, does grandma still love me and Suri." Tasha put her arms around her little man and said "Yes, of course she does. She loves both of you guys so much and she'll never stop loving either one of you."

Tears started to run down her face and she wished there was an easier way to deal with explaining her mother-in-law's condition, but the decision was made that the children were too young to understand. She never lied to her children and didn't want to make this a habit. "Mom she don't want to see us no more and daddy don't come home at night no more." Tasha was speechless and didn't know what was the right thing to say. She had told Face the children wouldn't know so she kept quiet and held her son tighter.

Just then little Suri swung open the door and said, "Mommy can I have a hug too." Tasha opened up her arms and gave her children a big hug and lots of kisses.

Washington, D.C...

A block away from the White House a tinted black limousine pulled over and parked. Moments later a grey Range Rover pulled behind it and parked. Paul Warner got out of his SUV and walked over to the limo, and then he quickly got inside. The Vice President and an unknown man were already seated in the back of the limousine, and the two were holding hands.

"Hello Vice President and how are you" Paul said, shaking his hand. "Let me get straight to the point. The President is not on board and will not have any part of this mission." Paul looked confused and said, "So we are on our own with this one?" The Vice President shook his head and said, "Yes, we are in this one by ourselves."

Paul looked over at the files that they had and said "How could he not consider this...he's a damn fool! Face had Watson killed and it's in the documents." The Vice President shared Paul's feelings but knew he had done what he could to prove his case. There was the business of politics at hand, and Paul didn't understand that. "I did my best to convince him but now we have to move forward on this. I will get you what you need to handle this but you must remember this is between us only. You cannot let this get out." Paul nodded his head and said "I just need a year and I'll have everything in place to make this happen."

When Paul exited the limo he got in to his Range Rover and smiled. He was happy to have made a pact with the Vice President and he knew Face would soon be nothing more than a fading memory. He started up his car and sped off down the road.

"So that's the man who's going to take care of all the committees problems?"

"Yes he is, he's very good at what he does. He has been eliminating our problems for years."

"He's handsome but did you notice he's missing his arm."

"Well I'm not interested in his looks and he's assured me his disability won't get in his way."

"Well he's still a cutie" the man said as he started to unbuckle the VP's pants.

The Vice President had gotten himself a new lover to take care of his needs. His younger lover was eager to give him blow jobs whenever they had a private moment, and now was the perfect time. As he pulled out the Vice President's dick he began to suck his it, and the Vice President could barely maintain himself. His new lover had the best mouth on him

199

that money could buy and he was happy to be his sugar-daddy.

As the limo began to pull off no one could see the exciting activities taking place in the backseat. Things change, seasons change, but people don't.

Chapter 42
Center City…

Parked across the street from Robbie's condo was a white cable van. Inside of the van were Quincy, Reese, and Kyle. They had been waiting patiently while two of their men had been behind the condo disconnecting cable lines. They were all wearing their black Comcast Cable Shirts and hats.

Robbie was watching the 76ers vs. Heat game while he lay on the couch relaxing. In the middle of the game the cable went out. He was pissed and jumped up to see what was going on. "Goddamn cable people" he said, opening the window because he noticed the cable truck when he was searching for the source of the problem. "Yo, get off y'all asses and fix the damn cable."

Robbie then slammed the window and walked back to the couch. He got his blunt and lit it up to calm himself down. He had finally gotten himself to chill and the cable guys had messed it up. As he put the blunt to his lips, he took a long pull and when he exhaled the doorbell rang.

"Who is it" Robbie yelled, getting up from the sofa and looking through the peep hole. "It's Comcast. We need to check your cable box." Robbie saw that the two men at the door were cable men and opened the door. "About time" he said, making his way back to the couch as the men walked behind him.

Without hesitation Quincy and Kyle rushed behind Robbie and pushed him to the floor. Then they both pulled out their guns and aimed them at his head. "What's going on" Robbie said. Quincy smacked him in the back of his head with his gun and said, "Shut the fuck up nigga. If you try anything you'll be dead before you can think of your first move."

Robbie had been turned around and he looked at his gun that was sitting on the coffee table. He now regretted opening the door without his weapon in hand. He wasn't sure who these men were and what they wanted. It didn't seem like they wanted to rob him because they weren't asking for money or looking through any of his things. In a desperate attempt to get the men to leave he said "Do y'all know who my father is" and to that Quincy responded, "Fuck your father."

Suddenly the door opened and Reese, Doc, and Face walked inside and locked the door behind them. Robbie saw his brother and he couldn't believe his eyes, knew he had fucked up. Face walked over to Robbie and looked at him as he was now sitting on the couch petrified. He hated who Robbie had become and when he saw how much he resembled Hood, his hatred grew even more.

Quincy and Kyle held Robbie down on the couch and Face leaned in and said "You fucked up when you shot my mom." Robbie didn't like the mention of Pamela, and as he struggled for his release, he said "Fuck her and fuck you." Face giggled and said to him, "Once I loved you. I really loved you as my brother and you go and shoot my mom." Robbie didn't care he was enraged. "Fuck you, you killed my father! And I hope your mother dies, I hate that bitch!"

Doc stood there filled with anticipation and he couldn't wait to get word from Face. Doc had his black leather bag in hand, and it was filled with his medical supplies; and he had a long syringe in his other hand. He knew Robbie was not going to walk away tonight and after he disrespected Face, he was ready to make his move.

Face wasn't in the mood to go back and forth with his former brother, it had been enough that Robbie had shot her. "I don't think I'll be seeing you anymore brother. Our bond is gone and you'll soon fade away too." Face began to step back and Robbie yelled, "Fuck you and that good for nothing bitch. I hope she dies." Reese slapped the saliva out of Robbie's mouth and drew blood. He hit him hard enough to calm down his rowdy behavior.

"It's cool Reese, Doc he's all yours." That was what Doc had been waiting for. He quickly moved in and plunged the syringe into Robbie's neck. While Quincy and Kyle held him down he again tried to fight off the men but the powerful drugs that were circulating through his bloodstream worked quickly and made him go numb.

In less than a minute Robbie was completely still and unable to do anything; he didn't even have the control of his eyelids to blink. Face sat on the couch as Doc prepared himself for the extraction. Quincy, Kyle, and Reese too stood back as they watched Doc unbutton Robbie's shirt. Then Doc began to sterilize his chest, as he wiped it clean and pulled out an extremely sharp scalpel and began to make his incision. The instrument he used cut threw flesh effortlessly and blood began to flow from the wounds.

Robbie could see what was happening to him but there was nothing he could do. He felt no pain and was unable to move. Doc requested a pan from the kitchen and Kyle had gone to get it. The removal of intestines and guts was too much for him. He had watched Doc use a device to break Robbie's chest cavity and he was ready to vomit.

Moments later Kyle came back with the a pot for Doc. Face, Reese, Quincy, and Kyle all sat there and watched in amazement as Doc pulled out Robbie's beating heart, and quickly placed it into the pot. Doc handed the pot to Face and said, "Here you go. Do what you like?" Face put down the pot and pulled out his 40 caliber handgun that was inside the shoulder holster underneath his black leather jacket. He walked over to Robbie and aimed at his head.

"Tell your father I said hello", he said, before squeezing the trigger. Bowww!!!Brain matter spread everywhere and the load bang sent a vibration through the apartment. Doc quickly asked "What do you want to do with this" he asked, holding the pot with the heart in it. "Doc, it's yours. Make sure y'all clean up in here-no traces."

Face and Reese walked out of the door and into the dark night. They had parked a quarter mile from the condo. It was a cold night outside and as they walked they were silent. Once they reached the car Reese asked "You okay Face". Face was silent for a moment and said, "Yeah, I'm good." Reese didn't believe him and said, "Brother or not, he shot your mom. You did what you had to do and that's it."

Face looked at Reese because what he was saying was true. He did have to get rid of Robbie and there was no other way to deal with him.

As the car started up, Reese began to drive Face back to the hospital. Now once he got there he could feel better knowing his mother's attacker was no more.

Chapter 43
One Week Later
Chester, PA...

Inside of a private location in Chester, PA- a small suburb on the outskirts of Philadelphia- Face sat around a table with five of the top drug Kingpins on the East Coast; Big Ticket from Boston, Mike Davis from Baltimore, Sincere Jones from New York City, Dirty Dank for Miami, and Frank "Underworld" Simms from Philly.

Face had guaranteed them all any amount of cocaine and heroin they could handle, at the best price in the world. Each had been a loyal and stand-up Boss in their own right, and they respected Face as a true leader and the man with the major connect. The meeting was short and to the point. Face was expanding his operations and he needed loyal, thoroughbreds to come on board and move weight.

The next day he was on a private plane with Reese to Las Vegas, Nevada. He met with a handful of Kingpins on the West Coast. The meeting was similar to the one he had the day earlier. He was expanding and taking over. He had no problem letting others eat, but he was always going to be The Boss.

Two Days before Christmas
Cottman Avenue & the Boulevard...

Face, Quincy, Reese, and Kyle were all inside a large warehouse, watching as the team of workers loaded kilos of cocaine and heroin into the secret compartments into the ambulances and luxury limousines. Face had invested in the purchase of twenty used ambulances and six limousines; as well as a used Greyhound bus. He had them all refurbished and they looked brand spanking new, and the bus and ambulances were tagged with the company name '*King Transit*'.

For the last few weeks, shipments of cocaine, heroin, and marijuana had been disturbed all over the country. Face had many people on his payroll, including state police, and bridge and toll employees; to ensure his shipments made it to their destination without any interruptions.

Face was moving more product than he had ever moved before. He was the number one distributor in the United States; and no one knew the full extent of his power except his supplier Roberto Fuentes, and Quincy and Reese. He was getting back into his business heavy but he didn't forget his main priority; his mother's health and rehabilitation efforts.

Pam was still going in and out of consciousness and occasionally she called out for Face. Her memory still had not fully come back. Face had no limitation on the amount of money he was willing to spend to get his mom back and fully operational. He had specialist flown in from California and Atlanta to help with his mom's recovery.

Face had been very busy but was putting in more effort to make it home at night so he could spend time with his wife and children. After Tasha talked to him about his son's request for more attention, Face felt bad. He loved his kids and didn't want them to think their daddy had fell out of touch with them. It was a lot for him to juggle but he was set on making it all work.

Mike Conway LLC.
Surveillance and Investigations
Manhattan, New York...

Mike Conway was sitting at his desk going through the files for his next case, when he heard a knock at his door. "Come in, the doors open" he said. When the door opened, Paul Warner calmly entered but he was holding a loaded pistol with a silencer attached.

"You fucked up big time Mr. Private Investigator."

"What are you talking about" Mike asked, as he slowly began to raise his arms. Fear was written all over his face. Having a gun pointed at his head was something he wasn't used to.

"You didn't think I would eventually figure this out?"

"Figure what out, what are you talking about?"

"Save it Mike. You should have never gotten that room next to Peter...you remember now, in the Hilton."

"What are you talking about?"

"You've been working for Face for some time. You gave him information that allowed my friend and his wife to be killed. You know exactly what I'm talking about."

Paul squeezed the trigger of his automatic weapon, striking Mike Conway multiple times in his head and chest. He died instantly and Paul began to rummage through Mike's office for information that would get him closer to Face. He took an empty box and began putting files into it from the file cabinet. When he was done he walked out as calmly as he had entered.

2:15 AM
Christmas Day
Villanova, PA...

Tasha woke up from a terrible nightmare and she was covered in sweat. Beside her was her two children who were sound asleep, so she sat up as quiet as she could so she would not wake them. She had dreamed that Face had been hurt and the nightmare had been so vivid and felt too real.

As she slid out of her bed, she reached for a small facial towel and made her way into the bathroom inside of her bedroom. Tasha wet the rag and began to wipe her face but she still couldn't shake the bad dream. She thought about calling Face but it was too early in the morning. He was at the hospital with his mom and she didn't want to wake Face.

Tasha made her way back into the bed with her children and as she tried to tell herself everything was okay she began to pray. She needed her husband to be alright and as the tears began to fall down her face, she softly said "God, please watch over Face." She held her children tight and did her best to fall back asleep.

Chapter 44
2:17 AM
Christmas Day...

The halls of Hahnemann University Hospital were quiet and empty. Those on the nightshift often dosed off during the early mornings when they had nothing to do, and today was no different. A young and beautiful nurse had just gotten off of the elevator and walked towards Pamela's room. Before she entered she paused, taking a deep breath and calming the fear that was running through her body.

Ever so silently, she entered the room and looked quickly to see who was inside. In the bed lay Pamela but in the corner near the window, Face was fast asleep in the reclining chair. He was bundled up under two white hospital blankets and he looked very peaceful. The nurse took another silent deep breath as she moved closer towards Face. Reaching into her handbag, she pulled out a 9mm that she had purchased some time ago. She had become very familiar with her weapon and although she had never hit a live target, she was ready to put her skills to the test today.

She inched closer to Face and with her gun in hand; she aimed her gun at his chest. She took a deep breath and she could feel herself shaking and she did her best to hold her hands steady. With the gun pointed at Face's chest, she closed her eyes and squeezed the trigger.

COMING BLACK FRIDAY 2013
JIMMY DASAINT PRESENTS...

BLACK SCARFACE 4

"LIVE A KING...DIE A LEGEND"

DASAINT ENTERTAINMENT ORDER FORM

Please visit www.dasaintentertainment.com to place online orders.

You can also fill out this form and sent it to:
DASAINT ENTERTAINMENT
PO BOX 97
BALA CYNWYD, PA 19004

TITLE	PRICE	QTY
BLACK SCARFACE	$15.00	_____
BLACK SCARFACE II	$15.00	_____
BLACK SCARFACE III	$15.00	_____
YOUNG RICH & DANGEROUS	$15.00	_____
WHAT EVERY WOMAN WANTS	$15.00	_____
THE UNDERWORLD	$15.00	_____
A ROSE AMONG THORNS	$15.00	_____
CONTRACT KILLER	$15.00	_____
MONEY DESIRES & REGRETS	$15.00	_____
ON EVERYTHING I LOVE	$15.00	_____

Make Checks or Money Orders out to:
DASAINT ENTERTAINMENT

NAME: _____

ADDRESS: _____

_____

CITY: _____ STATE: ____
ZIP:_____ PHONE:_____
EMAIL:_____
**$3.50 for each book to cover shipping and handling cost
($4.95 For Expedited Shipping per item)
WE SHIP TO PRISONS!!!**

Made in the USA
Lexington, KY
03 May 2015